DOMINIC MORALES

A Thousand Blades

(The Evolved, Book 0)

Second edition

ISBN: 978-1-958731-02-4

Cover art by Jesse Painter
Editing by Shire Brown

This book was professionally typeset on Reedsy.
Find out more at reedsy.com

Contents

1

6:30 P.M.

Days seemed to slip by in a hurry during the summer months. Students often watched their break shrink as the return to school lurched closer. Parties, sports, games, and camps only delayed the inevitable. There was no real way to stretch out the days to prevent the summer break from ending, but there were some students that didn't mind this fact. One of these students was a sixteen-year-old, Violet Woz, who had just returned from a three-month summer camp. She hadn't heard from her friend in quite some time, but that didn't bother her. She was in the middle of finishing her book and preferred to be undisturbed.

Violet breezed through her required summer reading during the first month of the break and was now rereading one of her personal favorites. She had always been a bookworm, so it was no surprise when she ran out of literature. Fortunately, her household was an educational environment with an extensive collection of reading material.

A significant portion of the collection came from Ivan, Violet's father, who kept all of his textbooks from college, as well as every research article he and his colleagues wrote. The documents were often filled with technical jargon that required a doctorate in bioengineering to understand. While Violet wasn't able to fully comprehend everything that was written, she still enjoyed discovering new concepts. Ivan had previously expressed his concern over her reading his most recent document, but that didn't stop Violet from trying. She made a point to confirm her parents' locations before entering her father's office.

Out of the two, Violet's mother was the most important parent to pinpoint. Claire could move through the house swiftly and silently. It was critical to the operation that she was preoccupied to prevent her from wandering. Violet had to stand by while the day came to its end, waiting for her mother to begin cooking dinner. The family's weekly menu was written on the calendar, and that day had a tedious meal that required Claire's full attention. Just to be sure, Violet casually walked into the kitchen.

She noticed her mother expertly cutting the dish's vegetables. Claire's wavy brown hair was tied up. Fair, tawny hands held the knife as it glided through the stew's ingredients. Her sharp chestnut eyes were focused on the cutting board. Violet knew from experience that Claire had just started cooking, and her window of opportunity was dwindling. She hurried to the living room to confirm her father's location.

Ivan was always exhausted upon his return from work. At the time, he was resting on the couch. His dark skin was full of wrinkles from both stress and age. Streaks of white peppered his black hair. He didn't say a word when Violet entered the living room. Instead, he increased the television's volume. The news reporter was describing a recent homicide. The incident occurred several miles away from them, and the perpetrators were missing. Similar reports were broadcasted earlier in the day. Everyone was worried that this was some type of terrorist attack, but there was too little information to make that assumption. Violet was unaware of these reports, so she couldn't grasp the scale of the events occurring. Ivan, on the other hand, grew more worried and thought about taking his family upstate. Against his better judgment, Ivan brushed aside the idea and waved Violet away.

With a slight bow, the curious child left the room and silently rushed to her father's office. Ivan didn't keep it locked but still expected his daughter to stay out. She was often well-behaved, but she'd act out as long as she knew she wouldn't be caught. Violet held her breath and pushed the office door open. She shuffled inside and closed the door behind her.

The office was a large room with towering bookshelves filled to the brim. Books were categorized and placed on the bookshelf along with similarly themed works. The topics ranged from basic medicine to highly advanced technical books, mostly adhering to Ivan's profession. Violet always thought this room was magical, but her main focus was the dark oak desk in the far corner. It was piled high with several stacks of recently published articles and documentation from Ivan's work. A "world's best dad" mug full of pens sat near the edge. Sticky notes were placed all around the computer's monitor. Each one noted a specific project or task that Ivan needed to remember. With little time and a need to reduce possible evidence, Violet carefully pulled a document from the pile. Her heart fluttered as she read the title.

The Materialization of Ichor and Genetic Variability of the Evolved. The title alone fascinated Violet. She didn't know what the document contained but was eager to learn. After reading for a few minutes, Violet realized she'd heard some of the terms before. "Evolved" was a label she'd heard from the news. It described a type of genetically modified organism that was altered to withstand harsh environments. The government had announced that human trials would begin at the start of the next year.

Violet was unsure how the testing would go. There were many groups who opposed it and vilified anyone that dared to volunteer for the trial. Many different concerns were raised, but they weren't enough to stop the project from moving forward. Violet was indifferent to the politics behind the experiments. She was more interested in the test itself and the results it would produce. The only question on her mind was how it involved her father.

Ivan was a low-level researcher at a local clinic. He was supposed to be currently researching the development of more-advanced artificial limbs, yet his notes littered the article. Ivan clearly had a larger role than what he described to his family. Violet continued to skim through the papers. She wanted to better understand the current state of the project. Images and descriptions of body parts, the variation of subjects, and an odd dark matter confused her. It was too much information to take in at once. Violet decided to retreat to her room for further analysis, but her plan was interrupted. A sharp snapping sound echoed through the room and snapped her out of her thoughts.

Immediately, Violet dropped to her knees and hid behind the desk. She was always quick to startle, but it often played in her favor. There had been many instances where her father entered his office to quickly grab something. Violet was caught red-handed the first time that had happened, and it didn't take long for her to learn from that instance. Now, even the slightest noise would cause her to hide. The best spot to conceal herself was underneath the desk. A large panel shielded her from anyone's sight, and small gaps allowed her to view the rest of the room. It always helped to see where someone was going and when they left. Violet squinted through gaps to better understand the scenario. A perplexing image filled her view.

A large, masked man in fine clothing had entered the room through the window. He stood almost six feet tall. Broad shoulders and a barrel chest formed his athletic physique. For an intruder, he was dressed extremely well. A black suit coat and tie matched with the man's slacks. A white button-up shirt was underneath his coat and was sullied with small splatters of blood. Everything was tailored to perfectly fit his body. Nothing about his apparel seemed to restrict his movement. Gloves and dress shoes covered the ends of his extremities. He would have been a remarkable bachelor, but there was one problem with his appearance. An onyx gas mask covered his face with pitch-black eye sockets. As the man scanned the room, Violet could only see the glimmers reflected by the room's light. It was like gazing at pure obsidian.

"All clear," the man reported with a deep voice. His words were muffled, but Violet could infer what was said. His polished shoes clicked against the wooden floor as he moved into the room. With the office door closed and a seemingly empty room, the man had little reason to conceal his presence.

Violet stared at him with wide eyes as he casually waltzed through the room. He slowly pried open the door to view the main hallway. As he familiarized himself with the house's layout, another intruder leapt through the window. The person's foot caught the windowsill, forcing them to awkwardly stumble into the room.

It was a woman wearing an outfit that was similar to her partner's. There were some slight differences. She wore a black vest rather than a bulky suit coat. The sleeves of her button-up shirt were rolled up to her elbows. Her porcelain arms, the only part of her body that was exposed, were covered in odd black markings that splintered into multiple smaller branches. Her clothes and arms were covered in a considerable amount of blood. Her menacing demeanor was exemplified by the midnight-black plague doctor mask that covered her face. A small hat made of the same material rested atop her head. The rest of her head was veiled with a black cloth. Muddy footprints trailed her as she meandered toward her partner.

"Are you alright?" the man asked his partner in a low voice. He closed the door to silently address the issue.

"I'm fine. Just a bit woozy. Might need a second before we take out the next target," the woman replied with bated breath. She placed her hands on the desk and leaned forward. Several deep breaths help her slightly regain her composure.

"Whatever it takes. Just do it quickly. We need to move on," the man stated as he started to scan the numerous bookshelves.

"Love you too," the woman laughed. She shuffled some of the papers on the desk. Many fell to the floor as she tossed them aside. It didn't seem like she was looking for anything in particular. She was simply passing time, waiting to fully recover. The room fell silent for several minutes before the woman spoke up. "So, we killing this bastard or what?"

The concept of murder taking place in her house caused Violet to gasp. It was a quiet inhalation, but Violet still panicked and covered her mouth with her hands. The atmosphere became heavy. The room chilled as time stood still for the hiding girl. She prayed that she wasn't detected, but to no avail.

The desk was tossed aside with ease, and the woman stared down at Violet. She couldn't see the intruder's eyes, but she knew she was being looked down on in disgust. There was nothing the young woman could do in this situation. Her voice was caught in her throat. Fear took over in an instant. Without a second thought, Violet flew toward the door. It was the fastest she had ever run, but it was not enough. The masked man blocked the door and grabbed her without hesitation. He threw her to the ground with an extreme amount of force and pinned her to the ground.

"A child? She wasn't in the report," the man stammered. He seemed to have been made uncomfortable by Violet's sudden appearance. The strength of his hold loosened but still prevented his victim from escaping.

"Too many targets and not enough intel. Regardless, she's here, so we ought to put her down," the woman retorted with a tired voice. She stood above her partner and glanced toward the document that Violet tightly gripped. A cruel heel pressed on Violet's wrist, forcing her to release the papers. The masked woman swiftly snatched the article and scanned it. After a brief reading, the woman shook her head. "Naughty girl. You shouldn't be reading this. Now you really need to go."

"No. We're following our orders to the letter. That was the agreement. This kid's got nothing to do with this," the man argued. The two intruders stared at each other. Not even their masks could hide the hostility in their glares.

"This isn't up for debate."

"I agree. Stand down. Now."

Violet could feel the overwhelming pressure the two radiated. She didn't want to be caught in the middle of their dispute. She needed a way to escape quickly. That was when a small glimmer of hope caught her attention.

"You don't have authority over me. Not here. Not ever," the woman's cold words cut into her partner. The two were equals, so there was no clear commander. It was because of this that the argument was allowed to continue. Their relationship was slowly deteriorating as their venomous words continued. It was thanks to this authoritative debate that Violet could subtly move her free arm.

"I do when you get like this, so shut up. If you want to kill someone, go deal with the doctor. He's bound to have heard the commotion." The man gestured with his head toward the door. Neither intruder would budge on their position. It was best to simply move on and hope one would forget about the problem. That was what the man was aiming for. Fortunately, his partner was not in the best mental state at the moment.

"Fine, but we're definitely talking about this later," the woman said before kicking open the office door. Her steps hastened as she moved toward the center of the house. The clicking footsteps grew quieter as she went further away.

The masked man sighed. He slowly turned his head back to Violet. As he returned his attention to his victim, he was surprised with a pen stabbing his neck. The desperate attack was enough to penetrate his defenses. The weapon she used wasn't ideal, but it should have been enough to force him off her.

Time seemed to freeze for the two as they stared at each other. The man's grip didn't loosen nor did it tighten. Violet remained pinned to the ground. Her hand still held the pen which was embedded in her captor's neck. Blood streamed from the wound and flowed down her arm. She was petrified with fear. The man was too surprised to move. Almost an entire minute passed before motion occurred.

The man gently pushed Violet's hand away. He nonchalantly pulled the pen and tossed it aside. His hand then moved towards his victim's mouth. He didn't cover it completely, so she could still breathe and speak. His movements perplexed Violet. Before she could say a word, something else derailed her train of thought. A sensation like a light mist brushed against her face. Violet tried to avoid breathing whatever was present, but it was a futile effort. She could only hold her breath for so long. A forced deep breath brought a wave of exhaustion. Despite the intense situation happening around her, Violet's eyes felt heavy. She didn't want to fall asleep, but it was getting harder to resist the temptation with each passing moment. Suddenly, it all clicked.

"An Evolved?" Violet managed to utter her realization. Her exhaustion made it difficult to think clearly, but it was the only logical explanation she could think of. Neither intruder wore body armor, showing they weren't worried about any type of resistance. Violet was not the strongest in the world, but the man's strength was unnatural. Then, of course, there was his apathy toward the stabbing.

It was her realization that sent shivers down her spine. The situation suddenly grew much more dire. If they were the same Evolved outlined in Ivan's documents, there was no way any of them would survive the attack. It was almost impossible to remove something that was designed with durability as its focus.

"You seem to know more than I thought. Doesn't matter. Soon, everyone is about to be woken up to the truth of what your father and his friends have been up to." The masked man seemed annoyed by Violet's words. An exhausted sigh escaped the gas mask. He pulled his hand away and dug into his coat. After retrieving a small steel blade, the man slit his wrist and quickly wiped some of the gushing blood onto Violet's neck.

"Wha—" Violet stammered with a soft voice. It was getting harder for her to form full thoughts, let alone sentences. She couldn't finish her question, but the man was able to infer her question.

"I don't know how much you know about us Evolved, but we're not all bad. Sure, that idiot isn't the best example. She's not herself at the moment. Another product of the doctor's actions. As for me, well, I didn't kill you. Just knocking you out for a couple of hours and making sure no one else picks you off." The man said with a soft voice. He continued to paint Violet's neck, making her false injury look much more serious. Once he finished, he took the bloody knife and positioned it close to her.

"Why?"

"It might be ironic for me to say this, but I don't want to hurt anyone. At least, not anyone that isn't a target. You haven't done anything wrong. In return for helping you, I need you to do me a favor. After you have shed all your tears and the dust has settled, grow up into someone that'll make a difference. This will never end if we continue down this road."

The man's voice faded as he continued to speak. He went on about philosophy and the struggle between man and God, but it all went over Violet's head. She could no longer hear him as her vision blurred. Heavy blinks slowed as she succumbed to her exhaustion. The lull of rest had finally reached her. It was impossible to resist any longer. The wooden floor wasn't comfortable, but that didn't matter. She drifted to sleep. Her final thoughts were of her parents. Praying that they'd be safe.

2

7:00 P.M.

Dinner and liquor was often the go-to choice to enjoy the end of a long day. A beautifully cooked steak accompanied by a cold beer was the dinner of choice for most people. This was especially true for Harvey Allston, who had just finished his fourth can. The smell of cooked meat filled his backyard as he grilled alone. He was masterfully handling the charred meat as he reached for a fifth can. It didn't take many of them to get him drunk, but it was the only night he could drink them in peace.

His wife and two sons had left for a brief vacation, leaving Harvey with the house to himself. This once-in-a-lifetime opportunity presented itself, and he was not going to waste it. He increased the volume of his portable speaker. Country music blared at an obnoxious volume, irritating his neighbors. Harvey wasn't interested in the opinion of others, so he sang along to his music without a care in the world.

Visions of amber fields of grain filled his mind as he imagined his old life. He missed the laborious days running the family ranch. Without it, Harvey lived everyday unsatisfied. He never liked living in the city, and the boring political job he had didn't help the situation. Sitting behind a desk and approving different research projects was not the life he wanted. He pondered for a moment on the importance of some of those projects.

Perhaps he should have given them some more thought. To him, it didn't matter. Anyone could do his job. Harvey was just unfortunate to have gotten it.

He didn't realize how his decisions would come back to haunt him.

Harvey's patriotic singing was interrupted by a loud crash. The noise had come from his house. It sounded like one of the front windows had been shattered. An intruder? In a neighborhood as safe as Harvey's? No, they had top-of-the-line security. The neighborhood was gated and had stationed guards at the entrances. Harvey couldn't believe it, but a shaded figure moved within his home.

The intruder didn't bother hiding their presence. They moved throughout the house with heavy steps. Many loud thuds resulted from several bookshelves falling to the ground. What they were looking for wasn't clear.

Regardless of their purpose, Harvey had no intention of interacting with them. In his younger years, he may have been able to win in a direct confrontation. However, time had not been kind to him. He wasn't the strapping gentlemen from over a decade ago. Not even the knife he carried would help him in a fight. With this in mind, Harvey opted to leave and call the police.

He left the music playing as a way to mask his movement. The plan was to draw the intruder toward the backyard while walking along the side of the house. As Harvey proceeded with his idea, he pulled out his phone. His fingers had never dialed a number so fast. 911 was called within moments.

"You have reached the Houston 911 Emergency Center. All operators are busy so please stay on the line," the robotic voice responded to Harvey's call. His body began to tremble as the words hit him. He'd never heard that message before.

"Is something going on? A widespread emergency?" Harvey thought to himself. A sigh escaped him as he exhaled deeply. He needed to call

again once he was at a safe distance. His pace hastened as the street got closer.

Several windows lined the length of the house. As he stepped past each of them, Harvey took care to duck under their line of sight. He could no longer hear the intruder in his house. They were possibly in the backyard. If that was the case, Harvey needed to hurry before he was discovered. Despite his heavier physique, Harvey's legs swiftly pushed him forward. The edge of the house was within his grasp, filling the man with joy.

However, his escape was cut short by a hand bursting through one of the windows. It grabbed onto his shirt and tugged him toward the house. Startled, Harvey could only react by swinging wildly. He stabbed the arm with the knife he held, but the attack wasn't effective. There was no reaction from the assailant as they pulled Harvey closer. To stop himself from being swept into the house, Harvey pressed his legs on the window's edge and fought back. He continued to pierce the arm with his blade as he pushed away.

Several direct hits landed, but none of them seemed to have any effect. Each wound leaked a small amount of blood and another dark liquid. The hits themselves felt like they were piercing several layers of protection, but there was no visible armor. Every attack grew weaker as the resistance became greater and Harvey's strength was depleted.

Another hand emerged from the window and swatted the knife away. It then gripped Harvey's shirt. Harvey braced to be pulled in, but he wasn't ready for the absurd amount of force he was up against. The assailant lurched forward and rammed their head into Harvey's. Only one of the two recoiled from the hit. As Harvey felt his head snap back, the hands that gripped him opened. An audible thud accompanied the man as he fell to the ground.

Harvey didn't have time to soothe his bruised rear. He awkwardly twisted his body and scurried away. His feet carried him faster than he expected, resulting in an odd stumbling run. He gathered his composure as he reached the street. His ragged breath showed that he was no longer the track star he once was. Too many years had passed from that time in his life, but it was the least of Harvey's worries. The weary soul turned his head to see if he was being chased.

The assailant had already exited the house and was pursuing Harvey with slow steps. The person was clearly a man with a toned figure. No defining feature could be found on him due to his outfit. Classy brown dress shoes matched the brown leather belt that supported his azure trousers. A white button-up shirt was tucked in and covered by a well-fitted navy blazer. Black gloves covered his hands, and a cloth made of the same material shielded his neck. Everything the man wore was tailored perfectly. It exemplified his appearance while not restricting movement.

All of the cuts that Harvey expected to see were nowhere to be seen. The small amounts of blood had disappeared without a trace as well. The blemishes to his suit were repaired faster than Harvey produced them. It was as if Harvey's resistance meant nothing. Almost like it didn't even happen.

Surprisingly, that wasn't the assailant's most outlandish feature. A large mask was protecting his face from being seen. It had a cobalt base with several golden gears of various sizes plastered onto it. Each gear ticked in a certain rhythm as a machine would. A large gear covered the left eye, and a mainspring covered the right. The gears worked together to wind the mainspring before stopping to release the tension.

Harvey could sense the danger emanating from this mysterious man. He knew he wouldn't survive a fight. Without a moment of hesitation, Harvey sprinted further down the street. It only took a few moments for him to be reminded of his condition. Heavy footsteps and ragged breath were enough evidence that Harvey couldn't run forever. Several other houses have passed, so it should have been enough. With a glimmer of hope, Harvey glanced behind him to see how far he'd gone.

Despair was all that gazed back.

The masked man calmly walked towards Harvey, knowing his prey wouldn't escape. Long strides propelled the man closer to Harvey with each step. There wasn't any sign of fatigue or hesitation. Despite the full suit and mask, the man was fine. He was able to chase Harvey as if it was nothing more than a casual jog.

An ominous aura radiated from the man as he approached Harvey. Harvey was startled to see his pursuer so close to him. He moved to run again but tripped over his own feet. All hopes vanished as concrete filled his vision. Harvey slammed into the ground and scraped his face against the sidewalk. The color drained from his face as blood began to drip from his cheek. The pain wasn't what frightened him. He had just fallen in front of the masked man. He lost the chance to escape.

"Please!" Harvey turned to cry his surrender but was interrupted by a foot slamming into his nose. The front kick had enough power behind it to thrust Harvey's head back into the ground. Disoriented, Harvey raised his head in a swaying motion. He couldn't comprehend what had happened. His blurred vision slowly focused on the figure that interrupted his plea.

"Harvey Allston," the man spoke with a northern accent. He stood over Harvey holding a manila envelope. Papers spilled from the package as the man threw it to the ground. They were work documents, stolen from Harvey's home. Each one detailed the different research projects that he had approved. The man bent over to retrieve one of the loose papers and held it out to be read.

Alteration of Ichor and the Evolved for Suppression Capabilities. The confidential document hung in front of the man that had signed it. Harvey immediately recognized the title. When the project was initially presented to him, several key figures were in attendance to further explain it. They discussed the many reasons for and against the project's approval. After the discussion, everyone in the room voted on the project's fate. The results weren't projected to be announced to the public for many months, but the masked man seemed to know all about it. The two stared at each other in silence for several moments.

"Are you aware of the significance of these documents?" the masked man was the first to break the silence. His voice trembled slightly with anger as he spoke. Harvey felt as if he was being looked down on in disgust.

"I. . . it was for the betterment of the country!" Harvey screamed in defense. He intentionally raised his voice to draw the attention of others. His only hope was to receive help from onlookers. The answer Harvey gave wasn't the best one to give, but he couldn't think rationally. He began to move slowly backward in an awkward fashion. The conversation continued as Harvey slithered away and the masked man nonchalantly followed.

"Why exactly should we care about your country? Are we supposed to be loyal dogs to the people that created us?" the masked man spoke with an irritated tone. His aggravation became more apparent as he hastened his approach toward Harvey. In response, Harvey glided away at a faster rate. The other documents were left behind to dance in the wind.

"You could be more grateful for it! Without me, you would've never existed!" Harvey shouted in desperation. He never thought one of his decisions would come back to haunt him like this. Retaliation only ever came in the form of political debates. He never encountered this type of situation, so Harvey attempted to play a sort of god or father role to save himself. His only chance for survival hinged on winning his attacker's favor.

"Our existence was never in your hands. Our alteration was," the man sighed as he increased his pace.

Harvey began to panic even more at the reply and retreated as quickly as possible. The backward scooch turned into an off crab walk as he tried to get away. Meanwhile, the man was now walking at a brisk pace. Any onlooker would have thought the two were a part of a comedy act, but this was no laughing matter to Harvey. The blabbering man was clumsily scratching his rear end against the sidewalk's cement with each step. The two continued their movements for a minute before the masked man suddenly stopped. Harvey noticed, but collided into something before he could take advantage of the opportunity.

"You do know that playing with your food is bad practice, right?" a woman's voice spoke. The voice was playful, similar to how one would be after a night of drinking. It startled Harvey, causing him to flinch in an overactive manner. He didn't quite hear the words said, but he understood someone new had joined the fray.

A ray of hope shone in Harvey's eyes. Perhaps they had come to save him. The hellish events that plagued the night would finally be wiped away. Harvey could go on his trip and forget about his job. His decisions could go back to being just random documents and not the evil figure that stood before him. Everything would now be better. Harvey enthusiastically turned his head and prepared to beg for help.

One look was all it took to delete that thought from his mind.

The woman's words finally sunk in, and Harvey realized he was sitting between three masked individuals. Judging by their apparel, it was safe to say they were colleagues of the initial masked man.

The new pair consisted of a man and woman who both ignored Harvey. They were too busy staring at their acquaintance, almost like they were trying to put a name to the mask.

The woman wore black and white formal clothing consisting of slacks, a vest, and a button-up shirt which had the sleeves rolled up. Her porcelain arms were blemished by long black markings that spanned the length of her forearm. Her overall appearance was quite charming, if the viewer disregarded the plague doctor mask concealing her face. The mask was accompanied by a matching hat that sat atop her head. The rest of her head and neck were covered in a dark cloth that absorbed all light.

The man was the object that Harvey bumped into. He was dressed in formal wear similar to what his partner was wearing, but a coat covered him rather than a vest. Polished dress shoes and combat gloves covered the ends of his extremities, leaving no part of his body uncovered. A black tie hung loosely from his neck but didn't divert attention away from the focal point of the outfit. A large gas mask covered the man's head. Every breath he took was heavy and puffed bits of smoke from the air filter.

Both of them had large blood stains ruining their outfits. The woman seemed dirtier than the man, but it was hard to compare the two. The man used his coat to hide most of the smudges. Meanwhile, the woman wore each blotch like a medal.

"Designation?" the man in the geared mask asked in a professional tone. The two men stood perfectly upright while the woman casually rested her hand on her hips.

"I'm Crow, and this is my boy toy, Smoke. We're with the assault battalion," the woman in the plague mask answered. Their unique masks matched their names well. When she answered, she tilted her head as if their names were obvious.

"I apologize for her behavior." Smoke bowed slightly as he apologized. He turned toward Crow, who had started checking her fingernails. "Please behave yourself. We're standing in front of the battalion commander."

Smoke pinched his brow. His exhaustion stemmed from multiple hours of working with Crow. The two couldn't be more opposite in how they held themselves. Smoke tried to remain as serious as possible. The commander was a role model for him, so he wanted to make a great first impression. Crow, on the other hand, didn't bother altering her attitude despite being in the presence of a superior.

"Oh. He's Tartarus? Hard to tell with the mask on. Plus, he's not as scary as usual," Crow laughed. Her playful demeanor stood out from the serious situation around her.

"Crow!" Smoke shouted at his partner. His mask couldn't hide the embarrassment he felt. Their quick banter and smooth conversation revealed a deeper level of their relationship. It was clear Smoke was familiar with Crow while she was in this inebriated state. He was accustomed to handling her, but he didn't want to do so in front of his superior. Thankfully, the commander was understanding.

"It's alright. I'm familiar with my subordinates and how they operate. Crow's composure deteriorates exponentially based on the amount of hemoglobin she's exposed to, correct? As for you, I believe you're capable of generating many chemical compounds ranging from isoflurane to cyclosarin," Tartarus responded in a robotic tone. His words felt like they were coming from an article he read in the past.

"Wow. Look at you and your big fancy words," Crow said in a sarcastic tone. Whimsical hands shook to emphasize her message.

Crow looked down to view her commander's target, who was silently crawling away. Her leg slowly raised as she brought her knee to her chest. A deep breath and a moment of silence were all she needed to focus on her next action. Putting all of her weight into a powerful lunge, she crushed Harvey's hand beneath her heel. A sickening crunch could be heard as his hand was shattered beyond repair. The victim cried out in pain before being launched into the street by a follow-up kick. Crow was extremely pleased with her attack.

Harvey wasn't a light man. His heavier build would have stopped him from experiencing the brief flight into the street. Crow showed that she, and her colleagues, were both monstrously evil and powerful enough to do as they pleased. Of course, Harvey knew this. He had been briefed on some of their potential capabilities when he first viewed the project. This reality left him whimpering on the street praying for a way to escape. If there was a way to stop them, Harvey would have been briefed on it. All he could do was clutch his bleeding hand as the predators moved closer.

"Her odd behavior may seem villainous, but you must remember that you approved of her alteration. You only have yourself to blame for this," Tartarus said smugly. He approached Harvey with soft steps, as one would a wild animal.

"Yup yup yup. I'm the queen of mayhem that's literally fueled by blood. You must be so proud," Crow said, circling Harvey. Her aura radiated bloodlust as she viewed her prey. She raised her hands above her head before thrusting them down violently.

As Crow's arms fell to her side, large spikes made of bone burst from her arms. Blood and a strange black liquid puddled around the thorns, but none of it dripped. The two liquids mixed and hardened around the ivory skewers. The new foundation around her arms was tough, serving both offensive and defensive purposes. With the formation of her new weapons complete, Crow held out her arms to show them off.

"I'm her partner, the one that is chemical warfare incarnate. It's a pleasure to meet the man that admitted me to be turned into a weapon. I've created several new chemicals just for tonight. I hope you'll enjoy them." Smoke walked the opposite direction Crow did. Several steps around Harvey led him to the perfect spot.

A dark mist began to escape from his sleeves and neck. It danced in the air as the wind blew. With Smoke's current position, the fumes were able to reach Harvey. The stream of gas suddenly became less dense as its production slowed. The cloud of vapor that passed Harvey dissipated, almost like it recalibrated itself to only attack the current target.

"Finally, there's me. One of the five commanders responsible for tonight's event. I'm the one that was imbued with some of the best combat capabilities among the Evolved. Then I was *blessed* with brutal training to become the perfect soldier. It will be my pleasure to be the one that ends your life." Tartarus reached into his coat and retrieved an odd T-shaped handle. It was made of a material similar to bone and had strange black etchings. It fit perfectly in Tartarus's hand as he twirled it between his fingers.

With a firm grip, Tartarus grasped the bone as it began to change. The complicated contraption extended from the top. The addition was several feet in length and came to a sharp point. Numerous smaller spikes formed along the central one, creating a silhouette similar to a pine tree. A black liquid, much like the one that appeared on Crow, oozed from the handle and filled the gaps between each structure. It quickly hardened once its shape was perfect. The blade had finished its construction and was ready for action.

Harvey was forced to watch in horror as his murder weapon formed before him. He was surrounded by three people who were currently considered to be weapons of mass destruction. All of them had the intent to kill and focused their sights on him. No amount of begging would spare him, but that didn't stop him from trying. Harvey slammed his forehead onto the street's pavement as he prostrated. His lungs burned from the smoke as he sobbed for forgiveness. Anything that came to mind with the potential to save him was shouted with a trembling voice. Tears dropped to the ground as he continued to cry. Harvey had never been a religious man, but he was praying to any god that would listen.

None answered his call.

Harvey, engrossed in his atonement, failed to notice the movement around him. The three were approaching but suddenly stopped. All of them leaped back as something new injected itself into the scenario.

The sound of a car horn was accompanied by screeching tires. The pleading shell of a man was unable to react in time. He could only see the vehicle through his peripheral vision before it filled his sight. The blinding brightness of the headlights froze him in place as the truck got closer. Harvey felt his arm shatter upon impact as the bumper collided with him. The vehicle screeched to a halt while its victim was thrown further down the road. The asphalt chipped away at his clothes and skin as the momentum scraped him along the ground.

After coming to an agonizing stop, Harvey rested on the ground for several moments. He painfully flipped himself to face the sky. The shirt he wore was torn away, along with several layers of skin. Blood fell from each of the deep cuts. Despite his best efforts, Harvey couldn't move his arm. No amount of hope would be able to drive his body away from these people. All he could do was moan in despair.

Several sets of footsteps approached the broken man. The masked figures all looked down on him in disappointment. None of them seemed to care about his suffering, but they didn't enjoy it either. Crow, of course, may have been the only exception, but she was now silent. She nudged Harvey's arm to check on his health. An angry groan was all she needed to confirm that he was alive.

Harvey wanted to crawl away, but it was impossible. The fear that yelled at him to retreat fell on deaf ears. It hurt too much to move. Nothing was worth the pain. All he hoped for was a swift end.

"Damn. I was really hoping this would last longer, but you had to get in the way of that. I hope you're happy," Crow said to the truck's driver. The engine was still rumbling as the driver hopped down from the raised frame.

"Sorry, but Tartarus and I need to get going. The situation has changed and we need to get our next target quickly," a new voice spoke. An audio modifier filtered their voice with static and echoes. It altered the voice to sound like it came from an old-fashioned radio. The new person was a man, but it was hard to tell from their voice alone.

"Understood, Commander Erebus. We'll stay back and finish here before moving on to the next target. Please, ensure that the mission is a success." Smoke said as he turned back and bowed. His statement had an intense sense of admiration behind it. The bow and title were more than what Smoke initially gave Tartarus, but it wasn't out of a lack of respect. It was more akin to a child meeting their hero for the first time. The vicious cloud that once flowed from Smoke had ceased and dissipated in the wind.

"What happened?" Crow asked in an irritated tone. The operation they were a part of involved multiple agents working simultaneously. Changing the order of certain events ran the risk of ruining everything. The night was meticulously planned. Any wrenches in the system needed to be addressed immediately. Thankfully they prepared for numerous possible scenarios.

"One of our prime targets has caught wind of our actions and is preparing to escape. We can't afford to conduct a widespread manhunt, given our limited resources. Tartarus and I will shift to Protocol 21. I already have my bases covered, so you two need to cover the targets he'll miss here," Erebus said, explaining the situation in a way that made sense to everyone. The authority in his voice went unchallenged by those who heard it. Smoke and Crow nodded in approval.

"Fine by me. Let me just finish this real quick," Tartarus agreed before crouching over Harvey. His victim was breathing heavily, and the light in his eyes was fading. Tartarus folded Harvey's arms over his chest. He leaned in closer to get a better look at the man that disrupted so many lives. "In the end, you really were just a man. Stuck in the past. We, on the other hand, have evolved."

Tartarus raised his blade, pointing it toward the sky. The black matter that comprised its edge shined brightly in the light. Like King Arthur pulling Excalibur out of the stone, Tartarus held the sword above his head for all to see. It would have been a beautiful sight if the viewer ignored the man that was about to be impaled. The moment they were waiting for had finally arrived.

In a swift motion, the sword was thrust toward the earth. The blade easily pierced Harvey's chest and hands. It even managed to break through the solid street beneath him. The color faded from the victim's face as blood pooled around him. A replay of his life's major event started in Harvey's mind. He wondered what series of decisions brought him to this end. At what point did it all go wrong?

Harvey wanted to think about this but instead offered a small final prayer. He prayed for the safety of his family. He had been so worried about himself that he never considered their current condition. Not even his worst enemy deserves this fate. Harvey could only hope and pray that the ones he loved were safe.

Memories of his wife and sons warmed his heart as he breathed his final breath.

3

7:30 P.M.

Staying ahead of the competition was the modus operandi of most news outlets. Information needed to be released quickly to the public. Of course, the content of an article was just as critical as its timing. Good reports could bring peace to a nation and provide insight into ongoing events. Bad reports could ignite rage in a person's heart or cause viewers to panic. Each report took a large amount of time and effort, especially in times like these. The world was on the cusp of change. Glimmers of a societal shift were on the horizon, but no one could have predicted how soon it would happen.

Reporter Julia Norris worked throughout her days, ensuring that every bit of information she wrote was authentic and beneficial. She worked at a reputable network that recently amassed a large audience. Her stories were always popular and often found their way into people's lives. In fact, it was one of her stories that brought the attention of many new customers.

At the time, Julia was researching information for her next piece. It was supposed to be an article about the most recent presidential press conference, but something about the story bothered her. The conference announced the start of human trials for an experimental DNA-alteration project. Everyone had their own opinion of the trials, but Julia was more interested in the validity of what was said.

She had several reasons to believe that the testing had begun months, if not years, before the announcement. To start, no official list of participants or registration process had been formed. Thousands of people were willing to donate their bodies to the cause, but nothing was being done. To add to this, there had been several skeptical reports released recently. They detailed the sighting of superhumans happening across the country. Apparently, average-looking people were seen performing otherworldly actions such as throwing cars, leaping buildings, and summoning weapons. There were even reports that these people were weapons themselves.

Of course, it was all nonsense. The world would have already turned upside down if it were real. Julia had no intentions of using these suspicious sources, but she still read the articles. They were able to serve as references for the horror story she was writing. She didn't believe in supernatural events or entities, but that didn't stop her from indulging in the tales that others wrote. She browsed through the different references before opening one to see the "real" story.

This one was different from the others. It did not explain its contents. Only a video sat on the web page, waiting to be played. Julia unenthusiastically moused over it and began the video. It was footage of a typical intersection, shot with an old security camera. The footage was mostly focused on the traffic, but many buildings were within the camera's view. The first few minutes proceeded as one would expect. Nothing interesting was happening and Julia questioned why this story was one of the most popular ones. As the recording passed the third minute, Julia moved to stop it.

Just before she could click her mouse, one of the buildings spontaneously combusted. A large fire started and proceeded to spread to the neighboring structures. Panic overtook everyone as people flooded the streets to escape. All cars had stopped in their place, and some drivers were even kind enough to leave their vehicles to assist others. After getting to a safe distance, almost everyone turned to view the fire. It was natural for them to watch this disaster. The building's flames flickered and danced enticingly. No one dared to move toward the threat. How could they? Nothing that they did would change the situation. It didn't matter. The professionals would soon arrive and solve the issue. All of the onlookers were content with waiting.

Except for one man.

This man rushed into the flames. The crowd was left shocked as they watched a hero in the making. The flames welcomed the running fool into the building. It swallowed him whole and showed no signs of returning him. Moments, which felt like hours, crept by as everyone awaited his return. Sighs of relief were heard as he escaped the fire. The man was leaning forward, carrying a weeping child in his arms. The girl's father hung from his hero's back, holding on to the man who dragged him out of hell. His injuries were more plentiful than the few that peppered his daughter. Without being able to escape, the father opted to shield her from the dangerous situation. Their savior, on the other hand, was uninjured. Only his casual clothing was severely burned.

Everyone moved to help the father and daughter. They took care to rest them on the ground before turning to the day's hero, but he was gone. He vanished in the seconds they looked away. Even Julia, who was watching the video from a high angle, didn't notice his disappearance. She replayed the video several times but couldn't find the exact moment he left. To the people in the video, it was like an angel came and quickly departed. They felt blessed to be a part of that moment.

Julia didn't believe that explanation. It defied all logic. Nothing couldn't be explained through facts and science, but she needed more information to prove them wrong. The story may not have been the most important at the moment, but it would be an interesting side article. Julia then decided to jump into this story. The conference could wait. She needed to shine a light on this event before someone else beat her to it.

Digging deeper into the video, Julia determined the location of the recording. A city named Ames quickly became her next target. The man she was looking for was a local hero and had been given the name Blaze. Several witnesses offered their opinion online, but Julia was sure to get more information from them in an interview. Not wanting to waste the opportunity, she spent the following days getting approval to go. It took a while to get her boss on board with the idea and secure the funding needed to travel across the country.

Julia's efforts paid off, and she had arrived early that morning. The sun was just rising over the horizon. The city's residents were leaving their homes. Fortunately, she was able to sleep for a few hours on the plane. To wake herself up, Julia smacked her cheeks and pumped her fist. She pulled her brown hair back so it wouldn't get in the way while running around town. It was finally time to hunt down a hero. There were multiple witnesses she needed to speak with, so time was of the essence. Anything the residents of this town said was bound to be helpful.

After a day full of questioning and collecting statements, Julia needed a break. She was at her wit's end from trying to find a solid lead. All pieces of evidence led to dead ends. It was all the same. "He was there, then not" was an excuse she heard multiple times that day. No one seemed to have a better story. It frustrated Julia, but there was nothing she could do.

The best option was to find a quiet place to reorganize her thoughts. When she finally noticed the time, her stomach began to rumble. Fortunately, Julia was able to locate a place that solved both of these problems. It was a small family diner located relatively close to her hotel. Not wanting to stay cooped in her room, Julia stepped outside and walked to the restaurant.

The restaurant wasn't particularly impressive. It was a standard building with generic decorations. The customer service was fine but not exemplary. Even the food left no lasting taste. It was the perfect neutral setting for Julia to reflect on the day. Aside from a random couple, the diner was empty. The staff didn't want to overwhelm their patrons, so they decided to stay back rather than wander between the tables. Only polite chatter and soft clinking could be heard. Julia's order was cooked quickly and brought to her. The mixed drink she ordered was the only oasis in this sea of mediocrity.

The few pieces of the Blaze-shaped puzzle Julia was trying to solve didn't quite fit together. She wasn't the first person to ask for more information. Everyone else who tried either gave up or continued the search from their homes. The evidence contradicted itself. Some of Ames's residents remarked that Blaze was a new firefighter that was just hired, but the closest fire station had no records of him. Few people mentioned his home on the edge of town. Many more stated that he was a tourist. It was impossible to push past all of the conflicting statements.

After finishing her food, Julia decided to end her train of thought. It would be best for her to relax for the rest of the day. Once the morning came, she'd be able to resume her work. Julia's mind began to wonder about her book. It was interesting that both her writing and her real life were becoming too fictional. She laughed at herself when she realized how far she had come to find a supposed superhero. It felt like she was the fool in her own story. Julia finished her glass before waving at the waiter and ordering another one.

The liquor halted Julia's thoughts. She knew she was susceptible to alcohol but didn't care. Her day had been a nonstop experience filled with air travel, tracking witnesses, and dead ends. Everything started to feel brighter as Julia giggled to herself. She started to think about how to enjoy the coming weekend. The newest announcement of the government's Evolved project had kept her busy. She pouted and thought about how long it had been since she had a proper vacation. Maybe she could spend the next day relaxing instead of chasing a ghost. Julia quickly pushed that thought away. She'd be in hot water for vacationing on the company's dime.

The waiter returned with Julia's drink, placing it near the table's edge. He was a young man who seemed to be just as lost as his customer. He seemed tired, but Julia wasn't sure if he was always like that. When she took a better look at him, she was reminded of the main character of her story. He was, for lack of better words, plain. Not as plain as the restaurant he worked in, but he was a close second. Everything from his height to his eyes was average. Julia didn't mean to compare the teenager to one of her characters, but it was hard to control herself. Her mind drifted toward the humorous idea that something she wrote became real. As she chuckled to herself, a shout grabbed her attention.

"Help! Please!" a woman screamed as she entered the restaurant. One look at her would explain why she was so panicked. The casual outfit she wore was torn in several places. Splatters of blood added color to her monochromatic apparel. The long black hair that hung from her head was jaggedly cut, resulting in a disproportionate mess. Her face was twisted with fear as she dragged another person into the building.

The woman was assisting an old man who seemed to be on the brink of death. His injuries were much more severe than his partner's. His professional outfit was destroyed and dirty, similar to the woman's. A large lab coat covered his body but had several gaping holes in it. His bald head had several cuts that were pouring blood. With the color drained from his skin, he looked like a corpse. Even his breathing had come close to a halt and was barely noticeable. One of his legs was visibly broken, which is why he required assistance. He limped alongside his partner, holding onto her for stability. He realized that if he fell to the ground, it would seal his demise.

"Ari?" the forgettable waiter called out. He rolled up the sleeves of his work uniform as he approached the two. He grabbed the wounded man and guided him. A table was cleared as the couple dialed 911.

"Freddy, do you guys have a first aid kit?! Doctor McElroy needs medical attention!" Ari called out. The doctor was bleeding heavily, so she was keeping pressure on the wound in his abdomen. Any assistance would be beneficial, but his survival hinged on care from a professional with the proper equipment. Thankfully, her cry for help was heard throughout the building. Three cooks emerged from the kitchen. One carried a first aid kit and gave it to Ari. She immediately opened it and instructed the cook on how to help.

Meanwhile, the other two cooks and Freddy turned toward the front doors. The three kicked open the entrance to confront whatever harmed Ari and Doctor McElroy. They were dumbfounded when no one was there. The only person outside was a random man walking his dog. The monster who harmed the two wasn't there.

"Maybe it was just a random attack?" the three thought. It wasn't impossible. Neither victim mentioned that they were being chased. It could have been a mugger who took the money and ran. No. Whatever hurt these two obviously had the intent to kill, but there was nothing these three could do without a visible target. They closed the doors and looked at each other. A sigh escaped Freddy as he turned to tell everyone the news.

"We're good. There's no one out—" Freddy was interrupted as he spoke. The sound of wood breaking rang throughout the room. A large, sharpened bone coated in an odd black material had pierced the doors. The spear shot straight through Freddy's chest before lodging itself into the far wall. Surprise filled the young man's face before he collapsed.

Moments of complete silence passed. No one could believe what they had just witnessed. Not even the two victims were ready. The people were like statues.

Julia was also frozen for a few seconds, but an interesting glimmer from outside caught her attention. Her eyes darted to the light source.

The flash was gone, but Julia's eyes widened. She dove under her table before a spear burst through the window. Glass showered the area around her, and the weapon embedded itself in the ground. Self-preservation kept her in her hiding spot as chaos ensued.

Spears began to enter the building in frightening numbers. Every window that faced the same direction as the front doors was shattered. The two cooks by Freddy were skewered, and the customer phoning 911 was pinned to the wall. Four of the spears that broke into the building landed near Ari and Doctor McElroy. Each of the spears grew thorns that extended several inches. The spiked javelins formed an odd fence that caged the two along with the cook that was helping them. Julia and the remaining survivor hid. The attack had finished, but there was no guarantee it wouldn't happen again.

The remnants of the restaurant's occupants slowly came to terms with what happened. The beast that attacked the doctor and his assistant were back. Everyone flinched at the sound of the destroyed front doors falling to the ground. When their collective eyes moved to the source of the sound, the assailant stared back at them.

It was a man equipped with one of the monstrous weapons. Standing over six feet tall, he emanated an air of arrogance. His high-class outfit showed that he was a step above everyday individuals. A copper blazer covered his well-tailored white button-up shirt. Black slacks stopped right before his perfectly polished dress shoes. While a stylish charcoal bowtie added to the classiness of his appearance, it was overshadowed by the oddity covering his head. A gleaming bronze Legionnaire's helmet shielded the man's head, and a mask was fixed between the helmet's side plates. Each piece of his outfit was cared for. It was clear that he took pride in appearances.

The man casually scanned the room, slowly pivoting his head. The clicks of his shoes echoed as he stepped forward. As the man walked, he tapped the spear along the ground. Each touch sent out a hollow sound.

It was unexpected given the apparent material of the weapon. When he first entered, the spear seemed to be there for support, similar to a cane. Now its utility was much more obvious to those who witnessed him.

The man was blind.

He used the spear to guide him, running it along the ground as he continued. His path stopped at the three trapped in the center of the room. Even without his sight, the man knew his victims were before him.

Julia froze in place underneath her table to stop herself from drawing the man's attention. She slowed her breathing and tried to do so as quietly as possible. As she concealed herself, she noticed the other customer doing the same. They were the only survivors who could hide.

The three trapped in the thorned cage were forced into the spotlight. Doctor McElroy rose to his feet but still needed assistance from Ari. The cook that helped them stood at the opposite end of the table. All of them were focused on the man who approached them.

"I know you're still alive. Had you let me kill you, I wouldn't have hurt innocent bystanders. Their blood is on your hands," the man said critically. He lowered his guard after taunting his target. The man was practically oozing pride. It was as if he knew they could do nothing against him.

The man's overbearing nature didn't stop the cook from fighting back. They lifted the table and swung it wildly. Plates and loose medical supplies crashed to the ground. The heavy object acted like a sledgehammer as it collided with the helmet-wearing man. Every ounce of the cook's strength was put behind the attack, but it was all for nothing. The man didn't flinch. In fact, he almost looked disappointed.

A swift kick sent the table flying, and the spear he held was used to slice at his opponent. A trail of blood danced in the air, and the cook's chest opened as a visible wound formed. They fell back, thrust by the impact of the attack. Sharp thorns pierced the cook's back as they fell onto the proxy cage. Little fight was left in them before they passed away.

Startled by what they just witnessed, the other customer yelped. Without a moment of hesitation, the masked man pulled his arm back before thrusting it toward the source of the sound. As his arm lost its momentum, a large bone erupted from his wrist. An odd black matter coiled around it and melded into the bone as it soared through the air. The end of the structure was eerily sharp, and it was perfectly straight. The construction was a perfect replica of the spears that had been thrown so far. Following the direction of the man's thrust, the weapon rocketed toward the frightened customer.

It took less than a second for the javelin to travel across the room. There was no difficulty passing through the customer like they weren't even there. Similar to when Freddy was executed, the customer stood in disbelief. Several moments passed before the reality dawned on them and they collapsed. The wound wasn't fatal, but it needed to be treated. The arrival of an ambulance was the only thing that would save them. Faced with a dire situation, hope was the only thing this person could depend on.

"Nope. Not those two." The man scanned the room once again. He turned toward the cage he made. "I don't enjoy doing this, but it's not like I can help it. You have to give yourself up if you want to save the others." The man's snarky remark only made the doctor feel worse.

Julia was filled with dread as she realized the position she was in. She was the only remaining survivor who hadn't been noticed. She was the only one who could save the two that were trapped. Julia had never been heroic, and the fear of death had halted her movements. She winced at the slightest amount of pain. It made her sick to think about a spear running through her.

She closed her eyes and tried to build courage. What could she think of that would inspire action? Who else in the world would thrust themself into danger? How did they do it? It all jumbled in her mind. The only hero she could think of was the man she was hunting for, Blaze. His resolve never wavered. He faced a monumental threat without allowing fear to control him. Maybe he was a cut above normal people, but that didn't matter. Julia was filled with determination. She readied herself to save the two captives.

To save them, she needed to confirm a few important details about the masked man. Julia silently lifted her arm and extended it out of her hiding spot. Nothing happened. Her arm slowly rocked up and down as she tried to establish a presence. The hand caught Ari's attention, but not the man's. The confirmation of his sight, or lack thereof, was crucial for her to decide her next action.

Julia brought her hand to the ground. Shattered glass covered the floor. Her quaking fingers carefully retrieved a piece of glass. A deep breath calmed her nerves as she brought the item close to her chest. With it between her fingers, Julia threw the glass across the room like a playing card. It flew in a straight line before shattering along the far wall.

Similar to his previous attack, the man gestured toward the sound's source. A spear followed his directional thrust with extreme prejudice. The hurled object hit where the sound came from, but the man was clearly dissatisfied. He didn't hear pain or the struggle for life that usually resulted from an attack. In fact, there were no sounds to be heard. Nothing changed. He missed.

Irritation quickly took over the man. His finger tapped the spear he held as thoughts raced in his mind. He lifted his weapon before striking the ground with its blunt end. The tile beneath him cracked from the blow. With an over-exaggerated motion, the man slammed his spear against the four that formed the central cage.

A hollow hum rang throughout the room when the two unnatural objects collided. Everyone sat in silence as the noise continued. It echoed off of the walls for several seconds before abruptly stopping. The man's genius was reflected in his action.

Once the humming ceased, the man twisted his head toward Julia. He moved to launch another spear but was interrupted midthrow. Doctor McElroy had tossed himself over the barrier that held him. He extended his arms to block the attack and push the masked assailant off balance. The doctor was too weak to do anything meaningful, but he was able to alter the throw's trajectory.

The spear that would have swept through Julia's chest missed. Thanks to the doctor's action, it was now lodged in the floor by her feet. She dove toward the sharpened bone and firmly grasped it. Small thorns that lined the shaft were invisible due to the coating material. Julia only noticed this now that her hands were bleeding. She wanted to release the spear but didn't dare to let go. All of her strength went behind a single thrust. The tip of the spear penetrated the man's defenses. It couldn't go deeper than a few inches, but that was enough. Julia put all of her weight into pushing the spear in farther. Doctor McElroy assisted the best he could, using the last of his energy in the process.

The masked man reeled backward, collapsing alongside the doctor. The helmet he wore loosely fell off as he bounced on the ground. Nothing was left to obstruct the view of his face. The first thing one would notice about him was how young he looked. He looked like a young man that was about to graduate college. The blonde stubble on his angular chin was properly trimmed. The hair on his head was long and swept to the side, covering half of his face. A large amount of dirt and dried sweat darkened his caramel skin. Cloudy blue eyes shined from the ceiling's lights. His lips were pursed as he reflected on what had just happened.

"Marvelous," the man said in a voice filled with fascination. He rose to his feet, carrying the doctor in his arms. Doctor McElroy rested limply. The life in his eyes had faded. His final heroic action may have temporarily saved the others, but it cost him his final breath. The man rested the good doctor on the ground with more respect than expected.

"To think that he'd give his life to save a stranger." The man tilted his head toward Julia. Hollow ringing sounded through the room as she dropped the spear.

"Blaze?" she stammered. It was the man she was looking for. The man that was glorified as a town hero stood before her as a mass murderer. Julia's mind began to spin as she reflected on the situation around her. She came to this area to look for a hero but found a monster instead. Everything she saw in the video was true. That was confirmed when she noticed his wound. It was gone in an instant. Both the fire and stabbing showed that he could survive anything. Julia's plan changed from rescue to survival.

"So you know that name? It is quite charming, but I'm currently going by Roman. I'd appreciate it if you'd call me that instead," the man responded, to Julia's bewilderment. He slowly bent over and retrieved his helmet from the ground. It took a bit of time to find, but he didn't seem to be in a hurry during his search. He left himself completely defenseless, turning his back to Julia and Ari. Neither of them had the courage to attack him, and he knew it.

"Uh . . . Roman, right? Why did you—" Julia tried to begin her series of questions, but Roman interrupted her.

"I'm simply following orders, darling. There isn't a real personal reason for this that outshines everyone else's. I just got a lucky assignment. Not much else to it." Roman grabbed his helmet and placed it on his head. With his face rehidden, he turned to look toward the remaining two survivors.

"Lucky?! Is it lucky to murder an innocent man along with several unrelated bystanders?!" Ari screamed at Roman. If the thorned barrier hadn't separated them, she probably would have attacked him. If she were uninjured, she would have taken whatever damage the spears offered just to hurt him. Of course, any answer he gave would have set her off, but the one she heard was the worst of all options. The traumatized woman couldn't comprehend what she had been told.

"Doctor McElroy was one of the most famous targets. Truly, he was one of the hands of God that created us. His developmental research on Ichor paved the way for humanity's evolution. Given that you work with him, I'm surprised you didn't know. He really was a gift to the world." Roman looked toward the deceased doctor. The words he spoke silenced Ari. She didn't know how to react. It wasn't a response she was prepared for. Julia, on the other hand, was ready for this encounter.

"What are you?" she asked, an obvious question. There was no doubt that Roman wasn't human, so he was an anomaly that needed to be explained. Julia's question may have seemed basic, but there were multiple reasons behind it. To start, she needed to build rapport with the man to raise the chances of their survival. Second, she needed to answer the questions that she prepared for the 'hero' Blaze. Lastly, she wanted to confirm whether or not he was involved in the government's ongoing experiments. It was fortunate that the man she chased loved to talk about himself.

"I am what's known as an Evolved. A creature created to surpass humanity in these trying times. Recently, I was altered against my will to spontaneously generate those spined spears and lost my vision in the process. Despite my blindness, I'd like to think that I'm one of the higher tiered members of the group. Maybe even the entire population, aside from those damned commanders." Roman gritted his teeth, thinking about those who could beat him. His pride stung every time he was reminded of the five people he could never best.

"The Evolved Test Trials haven't begun yet, and the test is supposed to change currently living people. Your creation story doesn't make sense. Volunteers are the only ones being altered, so you must have been a human at one point."

"I'm afraid not. I've been an Evolved since my initialization."

"If you really were created, why were you altered? What didn't your creators get it right the first time? Seems like a grave oversight to me."

"Humans have a hard time coping with the end of a project. There's always something they want to add to something at the last minute. Even though I was flawless from the beginning, the administrators still found issues with me. They wanted me to be modified to better suit their needs." Roman's narcissistic nature started to bleed into the conversation as it continued. He was irritated at the idea that he was altered in the first place.

"What needs could those alterations be useful for? No offense, but blindness doesn't seem suitable for an evolved species. You're leaving far too many questions without proper answers." Julia wanted to know everything. She didn't want to upset Roman, but it was getting harder to hold back her barrage of questions. Each answer sprouted numerous other questions. Roman mentioned a group, so he wasn't working alone. How many other Evolved are there? He mentioned assignments and other individuals that received less than favorable targets. How many targets have been placed? How are they related? She needed to know the scope of their operation. "You mentioned being lucky with your assignment. Does that mean there were others with terrible ones?"

"Don't misunderstand. Every target deserves what they get tonight. Of course, some targets are more favorable than others. Two of my close friends were unfortunate enough to be shipped across the country. I'd say I was lucky, given my target's identity and location. Sadly, I was only granted one target tonight, but I suppose it is better than those who didn't get one at all. With the doctor dead, my job is complete. I can sit back and watch it all go down in real time. Maybe I'll go find someone else that's free." Roman looked toward the broken front entrance.

Police vehicles had arrived on the scene while they were conversing. Blue and red lights illuminated the building as officers readied themselves. If he'd wanted to, Roman could have killed the remaining survivors. Instead, he casually walked toward the entryway.

"You're letting us go?" Julia asked an unnecessary question. In the given situation, it would have been best to keep silent. An average killer would reconsider their options and potentially revert their decision. She witnessed his face. She knew, roughly, his identity. There was no reason for Roman to leave them alive. Her question may have stemmed from curiosity and surprise, but it could have cost her life.

"As I said before, my mission was to kill the doctor. You and everyone else that died were just bargaining chips for him to surrender peacefully. My handsome face may have been exposed, but it doesn't matter anymore. It's not like you or the assistant will try to hunt me down if I leave you alive," Roman confidently stated. He acted like his actions were justified. He saw no use for the remaining survivors, so it didn't matter what happened to them. That said, Roman wanted to make one final dramatic statement. "Assistant, you must speak out against the improper practices the doctor and his colleagues utilized during my creation. I'm sure if you dig through his computer you'll find many juicy documents. As for you, reporter, I'd appreciate a well-written article about tonight. Something about how this was destined to happen after your nation's heinous actions. Instead of looking for me, do something you could actually accomplish."

He flinched as he ended his request. He realized he forgot something important. The helmet couldn't hide his embarrassment as Roman returned to the two. He retrieved a small handle from his coat pocket before swiping at the air with it. A long bone blade expanded from the handle, and an odd black liquid slithered around the blade before hardening. The weapon's composition was similar to Roman's spears. While they were comparable, Roman favored the ones that came from within him. He had more experience and was more comfortable with them. The blade he was now equipped with felt unnatural. The only reason he used this inferior weapon was due to the mission requirements.

Roman approached the doctor's corpse with the blade in his hand. A swift strike toward the earth pierced the target with ease. He paused for a moment, mumbling something under his breath. The sword stayed upright as his grip loosened. He took several steps back to get a better view of the scene. Satisfied, he returned to the entryway. Like a performer about to walk on stage, he began to psyche himself up.

Roman grew visibly excited as he approached the broken doors. He stepped outside and posed for the people there. The police officers trained their weapons on him. Several were holding standard pistols, and a few were holding rifles. The excessive display of force was meant to intimidate Roman. They believed he would surrender unconditionally. As they expected, he raised his arms into the air as he stepped forward with cautious steps. From Julia's perspective, Roman's red-and-blue-bordered silhouette resembled a painting she once saw. But unlike the solace that came from the historical artwork, his raised arms were not the sign of surrender. Her eyes widened as his steps clicked down the entrance's stairs.

Julia and Ari threw themselves to the ground as gunfire sounded. Bullets flew through the room. The front-facing walls of the building were riddled with bullet holes. The shots started at a steady rate but began to decline rapidly. Yells and screams soon replaced the firing as the fight took a swift turn for the worst. Last-minute prayers and cries for mercy were muted by brutal attacks. There was nothing they could do to stop the monster. As the last officer perished, silence filled the area.

Julia, motivated by curiosity, rose to her feet. Priority should have been given to the injured, but she needed to see what happened. She wanted nothing more than to see the fight's results. What kind of monster did she speak with? How little did he care for the humans that he viewed as inferior? Julia held her breath as she took one giant step forward and witnessed the end of a massacre.

4

8:00 P.M.

Late-night shifts were enough to drain anyone of their day's worth of stamina. People would arrive home exhausted from their long, backbreaking shifts. Weekends were an oasis that provided solace to those tired souls. Many people gathered together to share their time off and enjoy it even more. "Who had it the worst today?" was a question friends argued over at length. It was a common experience that most social groups competed over. The "luckiest" of these individuals were those that worked in intense professions.

One example was medical personnel. Doctors weaved their way through a large number of patients each day. Twelve-hour shifts were the norm for over half of the nurses working throughout the nation. Emergency room surgeons operated under stressful conditions. The work they did saved lives, but tonight would be their ultimate test. A wave of patients flooded hospitals all across the country. Terrorist attacks were occurring everywhere with little or no warning. No region was safe. Even the most remote hospitals began to fill. The limited resources these facilities had to offer were strained under the pressure.

The trouble came from patient organization and protection. Some of the less fortunate cases were registered as potential targets of the terrorist organization. These targeted individuals were relocated to secure sites where they would be treated. Everyone else was kept to their local hospitals. These people were random bystanders who got swept into the night's chaos. Their stories presented first-hand knowledge of the heinous creatures that spread terror to all who saw them. The Evolved were no longer distant, augmented humans. They were now the demons that couldn't be stopped.

Both law enforcement and medical staff were overwhelmed by the surge of calls made. There were too many issues to be resolved, and not enough people were available to help. If it was an isolated incident, other areas could send additional aid. Extra supplies and even some staff could be sent to provide relief. Unfortunately, the chaos started in heavily populated areas. This forced everyone's attention to these major cities. It left almost nothing for the neighboring towns that were also impacted. Pandemonium engulfed the country within hours. The agents of anarchy that started all of this roamed the streets without caution. Their endless motivation drove them toward their targets, killing anyone that tried to stop them.

Preachers spoke about demons rising from the ground and the downfall of the faithless. Politicians blamed the opposing party for the problem. Conspiracy theorists claimed that aliens arrived from outer space to retrieve their fallen comrades. Everyone was using the night to push their agendas, spinning their wild stories to fit a specific narrative. The small lines that divided people grew as suspicion set in. Questions popped into everyone's mind about who to trust and what to do. In reality, the answer was simple. The horrors that brazenly rose from the shadows only cared about their targets. If a person wasn't targeted, they only needed to stay out of the way.

The work of saving those targets fell upon police officers and the recently activated National Guard. They strived to provide protection to their local areas. Unfortunately, it was impossible to predict where the next attack would occur. They could only respond to the disasters as they occurred. In the few cases when they did arrive on time, the opposition they faced was outrageous. Standard firearms had no effect against them. Large weapons were a necessity, but even those weren't always effective. Questions arose about how to deal with the Evolved.

A basic understanding was starting to develop about these creatures. They were extremely powerful and diverse at the same time. Some were tougher than others. Some were stronger. Some wielded weapons, and others were the weapons themselves. Information on sighted Evolved was key to their elimination.

Meanwhile, the lives of those injured rested on medical professionals. Nurse Angelo Hernandez was one of the thousands called upon for additional assistance. He had just gotten off his previous shift a few hours prior, so it took every ounce of will power to return to work. His return was met with a surplus of patients in need of urgent care. Medical supplies would quickly become scarce if patients continued to spill in at the current rate, but Angelo couldn't stop their arrival. All he could do was help heal their wounds.

The injuries patients suffered from varied. This was due to the multiple types of Evolved that attacked them. None of them attacked in the same way. Poisonings, lacerations, stab wounds, and broken bones were just a few examples of what the people experienced. To add to the confusion, many wounds came with an abnormal black matter. In its liquid form, the substance had a consistency similar to honey and clung to anything that touched it. As a solid, it was extremely tough and required a large amount of effort to safely remove. Any portion of the patient that was covered in this matter was immediately cleaned.

Those that cleaned these injuries were surprised to see this material seemed to be healing the patient. The matter dissipated while accelerating the healing process. It was a miracle and saved many lives. Despite this, most medical professionals opted to remove the black matter. Temporary benefits were fine, but they feared the longer-term consequences.

In a way, Angelo was fortunate. His region only reported the presence of one Evolved, so most patients sustained the same inflictions: lacerations and stabbings. Many of the wounds were superficial and didn't require a large amount of attention. Few were extremely severe cases, and even fewer involved the black matter. It was an interesting scenario everyone found themselves in. The city's unstoppable serial killer was on the loose, but they didn't deliberately go out of their way to harm bystanders. People were only hurt if they tried to interfere.

One of these patients was Olivia Turner, who tried to protect her friend during an attack. She was having dinner with her coworkers when a masked woman appeared. One of Olivia's friends was targeted by the rogue individual. She did what she could to protect everyone, but it was impossible. She was a petite woman who had never been in a fight before. Facing an Evolved was suicide. It was pure luck that she survived.

The masked woman was overwhelming. The blade she wielded cut through anyone that tried to stop her. She didn't have any unnatural gimmicks mentioned in other reports. There were no superpowers aside from superior strength and agility. Compared to the others, this Evolved was of a lower tier. That didn't mean she was weak, but there were certainly stronger ones roaming the neighboring cities. The woman still managed to eliminate her targets despite this fact. She even hummed a lovely song as she nonchalantly took the lives of her targets. No one could argue that she wasn't still a monster.

Olivia woke up sometime later, meeting Angelo in a recovery room. She told her story as he listened closely. He couldn't imagine what the experience was like, but the summaries gave him glimpses into the night's reality. Like every other patient in the hospital, Olivia was visibly distressed. Angelo and the rest of the staff tried to assure them that they were now safe, but it was impossible to promise that. The hospital was not prepared for an Evolved to infiltrate the building. Whether by brute force or stealth, there was nothing to stop them.

Several police officers were on the premises, but everyone knew they were there as a security showcase. Two of them were interviewing witnesses. Any bit of information had the potential to save lives and prevent other targets from being eliminated. Olivia tried to help as much as she could. A facial description would have been the best possible outcome, but the woman's mask never came off. She was of average height and build. The only discernible feature about her was her obnoxiously formal outfit. Without it, the woman would blend into any crowd. Olivia didn't want to think about that. She feared the possibility that they would cross paths again without her knowing. The face of her friend being slaughtered popped into her mind. The officers ended their interrogation as tears trickled down her face.

Olivia bawled for several minutes. The room felt empty. Her heart felt heavy. Time seemed to halt as everything around her crumbled. The halls filled with the cries of the injured. Each patient shared the same level of fear. They could never return to their normal lives. A simple shift in the shadows was all it took to startle them. As long as monsters walked among them, they would never be safe.

Angelo softly knocked on Oliva's door before entering the room. He needed to change her bandages and see if she required further aid. Worried about her mental state, he tried to start a conversation. She was unresponsive to the first few questions. Her mind felt too numb. It took multiple attempts to break through her shell. They spoke about the most random topics to pass the time. A bond began to form between the two, and the room suddenly felt a lot less empty.

"So, you're a psychologist?" Angelo asked as he checked Olivia's vitals. His deep voice only added to the intimidating character he presented. Along with his voice, his darker skin and short cut hair drew the attention of less than desirable individuals. Fortunately, he was tall and well-built.

An intimidating stare and the right words were all it took to dishearten an opponent. Not many people wanted to be near him based solely on his appearance. Despite this, Angelo was an extremely kind-hearted man. He'd gladly give the shirt off of his back to help someone.

"Yeah. I've helped my patients through their troubles, but I never thought I'd face a similar diagnosis. This night will haunt me for the rest of my life." Olivia's soft voice trembled as she spoke. Her arms were covered in medical gauze. Her crimson hair rested lightly on her shoulders. Delicate hands held her arms as she continued to console herself. Downcast hazel eyes worried for her safety.

"'Progress is made one step at a time.' At least, that's what my shrink tells me." Angelo tried to lift the room's mood. He wasn't a professional at easing a person's mental trauma, but he spent the night trying to help the best he could. Not knowing the demons that haunted their nightmare, he could only help them at a basic level.

"True, but time is relative. Grief can make a person feel like they're stuck in place." Olivia was a realist. She never looked at the brighter or darker side of a situation. Everything needed to be objective. Of course, she would always offer help to her patients, but helping herself seemed like a futile effort. She knew she needed the assistance of another psychiatric professional.

Her eyes grew heavy. Her growing exhaustion demanded attention. Olivia shook her head. She didn't want to fall asleep, but it became difficult to fight against the lull of rest. Even Angelo felt its influence, which he found odd. Angelo had a habit of staying up late due to work. He shouldn't have been anywhere close to feeling tired.

"Given the reports, I can't blame you. It'd be one thing if that was an isolated case, but the Evolved are appearing throughout the country. We don't even know how many there are or how to stop them. The whole situation feels—"

"Hopeless." Olivia finished Angelo's sentence. They didn't want to ramble about discouraging topics, but it was hard not to talk about it. It was natural to mention something so important.

Curiosity grew in Angelo as time passed. Why did the Evolved exist when their development was scheduled for the following year? Why did they have enmity toward specific people? From his perspective, there was no clear answer. No connection could be made between targeted individuals. Even where exactly the Evolved came from was a mystery.

The two fell silent. The conversation didn't have any seamless transitions to another topic. Angelo's mind raced for something else to talk about. He didn't want to leave on a negative note. He tried to speak but stopped as he looked at Olivia. She was sound asleep. Her breathing had calmed, and she was at peace.

Not wanting to bother the sleeping patient, Angelo got ready to leave. He quietly stepped toward the door and reached for the knob. He thought to himself about the situation. A surplus of patients filled the rooms. The medical staff was working diligently to assist everyone that came in. People were forced to deal with the black matter that no one understood. It was hectic, to say the least.

Angelo readied himself to reenter his battlefield but froze. He noticed something strange. There wasn't chaos on the other side of the door. The cries that had filled the halls were silent. The entire building was eerily quiet. Everything had stopped. Angelo felt like he was just transported to an empty hospital. He pressed his ear against the door to hear what was going on.

All that could be heard was a slight hissing noise and someone humming a tune.

Stress began to build within Angelo as the song crept toward the door. He clutched his chest and stepped away. Footsteps clicked as a shadow formed in the door's gap. Angelo held his breath when the figure stopped. It stood at the room's entrance for several moments. A loud metallic clang echoed through the hallway. The hissing became louder as the figure walked away.

A modest puff of smoke wormed into the room from where the figure once stood. It crawled through the room at a snail's pace. The heavy mist hugged the ground as more continued to pour in. Angelo quickly panicked and backed into the room's farthest corner. He tried to wake Olivia. It may not have been the best option, given her trauma, but they needed to find another location to rest. Unfortunately, she wouldn't rise from her slumber. A cloud covered the room's floor in less than a minute. It was thick enough to engulf Angelo's feet but didn't hinder his mobility. He turned his head toward the door.

There was a high probability that everyone else was asleep. Whoever was skulking in the halls was almost certainly an Evolved. If one of them was here, that meant they were hunting a target. Nothing could stop them, but that didn't mean they couldn't get distracted. The hospital was full of patients from all sorts of backgrounds. A register of where each one was located would be locked due to security concerns. The one thing that was needed was the perfect distraction.

"If I pull their attention, I can buy the building a few minutes. Here's to hoping the security is doing check-ins like they promised," Angelo thought to himself for a moment. He took a deep breath before stepping toward the door. Was he about to confront a monster? What could he do against an Evolved? It was essentially suicide, but he grasped the doorknob, nonetheless.

The turn was agonizingly sluggish, and the push was just as slow. The smoke waved away but quickly rushed back into place. Angelo stepped outside. A metal capsule collided with his foot midstep. As it rolled away, its pores were exposed. The device was producing the gas that flooded the building's floor at an alarming rate. Unsure how to proceed, he turned toward where the figure should have been.

With the lights off, it was difficult to make out many details. A woman was crouched further down the corridor. Her silhouette was sharpened by the formal outfit she wore. A tie hung loosely from her neck and swayed as she worked. Given her height and humming, she was likely on the younger side of the spectrum. Her face was covered in a mask, but its interesting design was obscured. The young woman was facing away from Angelo, so he couldn't see all of her minor features. She carried two capsules that matched the one on the floor. A soft twist caused them to open with an audible snap before spilling mist onto the ground.

The woman tossed one of the canisters forward. A clamorous metallic noise rang through the hall once it landed. It bounced several times before rolling to a stop. Satisfied with its placement, the woman twirled elegantly. The mist circled her as she pulled her arm back to throw the next capsule in the opposite direction. Instead, she froze. Her humming stopped the moment she saw someone standing in front of her. They stared at each other for several moments.

Angelo was the first to take action. He dashed away. The steps he took were heavier than usual. It felt like he was carrying a significant amount of extra weight while running. Despite this, he pushed forward. He planned to draw her away. A quick turn split the two parties, and the woman slightly increased her pace. She didn't seem too enthusiastic about chasing him. To her, it was more like running after a ball rolling down a street. Her pursuit lacked the intensity that Angelo originally feared. If it continued at this rate, he may be able to survive more than a mere few minutes. She was getting closer to him with each step, so he burst into another room before slamming the door shut. The steps stopped before the door.

"Is she going to break it down?!" Angelo panicked. He dove to the room's window. His hands fumbled with its lock. Such a simple process was now the most strenuous procedure.

"Hello?" a childish voice spoke from the other side of the door. Several knocks shortly followed, causing the thin barrier that separated the two parties to rattle. Angelo stayed silent as he worked on his escape route.

He refused to respond, so the woman continued to speak. "I know you're there. Why did you run? I can help if you're hurt."

"Help?" Angelo mumbled. His words escaped him. The voice was enough for the woman to confirm his presence. She was curious whether he had a hidden escape route, but the conversation guaranteed he hadn't disappeared.

"Yeah. I'm sure you see the mist. It's a special compound from one of my friends," she answered. Her voice was friendly, but that didn't change what she was. One wrong move could end the nurse in an instant. The closed door offered no protection from such a monster. If she wasn't merciful, it would have already been removed.

"What does it do?" Angelo asked. He wanted more information. The woman behaved differently than he expected based on the stories he'd been told. She wasn't a different person. Her outfit, physique, and humming were all similar to what was stated in the reports. The only difference was her apparent kindness.

"It dulls pain, reduces inflammation, and increases the rate of production of collagen and granulation tissue. I'm sorry, I don't know much more than that. If you need further assistance, I can help you further." The doorknob began to shake.

"No! No. I'm okay. Everyone here is okay. Please just go." Angelo needed to keep her out. The window was finally open, but he was waiting for the right moment to escape. He thought of ways to stall the conversation. His mind strained for the words to say, but there was nothing. Pressure began to build as his voice was caught in his throat. He prepared for the worst.

"Oh. Sorry," the woman sulked. Moments passed, but it felt like an eternity to Angelo. The shadow under the door hadn't moved. The woman tried to speak once again. "I'm Sapphire. What's your name?"

"Angelo." He didn't know why he answered. Even if she was earnest and wanted to help, she couldn't be trusted. All of the Evolved were massive threats. It was foolish to attempt to reason with them. The only reason Angelo answered was that he didn't want to upset Sapphire. It was best to delay her from relocating, so he tried to probe her for more information. "Is Sapphire your real name or the one you're using tonight?"

"It's only for tonight. Sorry, I'm not allowed to tell you my real name," she spoke in a dismal voice. She didn't seem to like the secrecy, and her apologetic nature made it hard to antagonize her. There was no malice in her voice. The earlier chase could have been much worse. Angelo started to have an internal debate about her true nature.

"Who told you to use a different name?" Angelo wanted to know more about the Evolved and their hierarchy. Sapphire had answered his questions so far. It bought him plenty of time for help to arrive, and it aided his understanding of the night's villains.

"My commander, Gaia, told me to use the name, and my sister also warned me not to talk to humans." Sapphire sounded disappointed that their contact was limited. Her voice implied that she wanted to continue the conversation. The orders she received were the only thing that stopped her.

"If you're not supposed to, why are you talking to me?" Angelo tried his damndest to learn as much about the Evolved as possible. Any bit of information to increase his chances of survival was worth the risk.

"I was worried you were hurt. Like I said before, I'm here to help. The gas is putting everyone to sleep and healing them. The only reason you're awake is that you're in pain. It's either that or . . ." Sapphire's voice began to drift off. The shadow beneath the door shifted as she turned. ". . .Something else was keeping you awake."

"Why would you help? Didn't you hurt h—me?!" Angelo lied through his teeth. He needed to grab her attention. He would do whatever it took to protect Olivia from her nightmare. He figured it would be better to die a hero than a coward, not to mention his growing fondness for his new companion.

"Huh? I'm sorry, Angelo. I'm a part of the support battalion, so I haven't hurt anyone tonight. Maybe you've got the wrong person?" Sapphire seemed genuinely confused by his comments. Her confusion perplexed Angelo. All reports on the Evolved detailed brutal attacks. Not one mentioned a group of them healing the injured. It didn't make any sense to him. Why would they attack people then heal their victims?

"There's no way I'm wrong. You're the one that was humming when she killed my friend, aren't you?" Angelo had a bad taste in his mouth. It bothered him that this woman was such an anomaly. If her words could be trusted, she wasn't hunting a target. Her goal was to heal the people that were indirectly hurt by the targeted attacks.

Was it a sort of mutiny? No. She clearly had high regard for her commander and the orders she was given. So, she must have been ordered to heal. The earlier-mentioned support battalion confirmed that the Evolved split themselves into different groups. Was each group working independently? Did the groups have conflicting interests? There were too many questions in Angelo's mind. He couldn't keep up with it all. The growing exhaustion only made it more difficult to comprehend. Oddly enough, it would have been easier to understand if Sapphire was simply a homicidal maniac. Why did there have to be a group that was different to this degree?

"Humming? Oh, do you mean the Song of Healing? It's a song Doctor Woz taught me and my sister a couple of months after our initialization. He never said where it came from, but Mel—Ruby and I sing it all the time." Sapphire seemed energized by the new topic. Her fondness of the tune and the man that taught it to her showed. The excitement almost caused her to reveal Ruby's real name, but she caught herself.

"What's the Song of Healing? Who's Doctor Woz?" Angelo tried to comprehend the information that was dumped on him. There were too many new concepts that were introduced to him. He vaguely remembered a song with the same name from a video game, but he had never heard of the doctor. Searching his brain for further insights was pointless. Luckily, his first-hand source was willing to expand on what was said.

"It's just a song. Like a lullaby that the doctor taught me. He was responsible for overseeing a lot of us, but he was especially fond of my sister and me. I think someone mentioned it was because we reminded him of his daughter, but it's hard to remember."

"Why is it hard to remember? Does it have to do with the 'initialization' thing?" Angelo felt like he was getting close to an answer. He tried to fight the exhaustion that gnawed at his mind. It took everything to stay on his feet. The raw determination that kept his eyes open started to falter.

"Most of my memories are hazy when it comes to my initialization. There's not really a word to better explain it. I guess birth is the closest thing, but I was never really born. None of us were. I was never a baby or a child, and I don't have any parents. It's the main reason we use a special word for it."

"*Never . . . born? What does . . .*" Angelo tried to continue his thoughts. His legs lost their strength. The mist danced around him as he fell. The shadow beyond the door didn't move. Sapphire must have understood what was happening.

Angelo couldn't move. The fumes had finally taken effect. His vision turned hazy. Breathing became an enduring task. Sleep was forcing its way into Angelo's mind. Lying on the ground, he was swallowed by the vapors, so it only became harder to resist.

Sapphire didn't move. She listened patiently. Enough time passed for the last person to soon fall into a deep slumber. She began to hum the song she once sang earlier. Her immature voice dissipated as she continued with a tender tone. It was a lullaby that rested the weary souls of those that listened to it. The song filled the halls as she increased her volume. This time, the song carried a different message. Its rhythmic tune caught in Angelo's head as his eyes closed.

He saw the glimmer of hope that Sapphire was trying to convey. Tragedies required restoration, and restoration led to new beginnings. From a human perspective, tonight was a night filled with needless bloodshed and terror. It would be an event spoken about for generations. Nobody would be able to rest easy knowing of the perpetrators behind the night, but Angelo reflected on what that meant for the other side. Sapphire and her battalion were a sign that not all Evolved were evil. Thinking about it some more, none of the Evolved deliberately attacked anyone that wasn't a predetermined target. Everyone in the hospital was a victim of circumstance or heroism.

A connection was made between the two. Angelo began to understand the struggles of each Evolved. Sapphire felt sympathy for the fear humans had of the presence of new power. She understood because she too felt powerless against monsters at one point. It was those defenseless months filled with the alteration of one's self that motivated them. Angelo could almost see a frightened child surrounded by reluctant doctors in a white voided room. He thought about the black matter and how it played into everything. At some point, the truth would be revealed.

For now, all he could do was rest.

5

8:30 P.M.

The southern portion of the nation was known for its deserts and canyons. The intense dry heat was enough to fry an egg on the side of the road. Heat advisories became a daily norm in the summer months, but the locals didn't need to be told that it was hot outside. Fortunately, the sun had dropped beneath the horizon. Everyone was able to exit their homes as the temperature dropped. Many animals did the same, as it was finally time to feed. While they did explore their territory, the animals were limited to small areas.

Between the expanding technological cities were patches of forests and empty plains. These areas were the only refuge the wildlife had. With this in mind, the local government had several environmental preservations that were protected by law. Citizens were allowed to explore them, but it was illegal to alter the area in any significant way. Those that wanted to get away from the continually advancing world would move close to these areas. Many of these established residents were fond of nature, but some only settled there for privacy concerns.

Given the time of day, it was rare for anyone to be exploring the area. It was even rarer to see ill-equipped hikers marching through nature with little fear. Visitors were expected to bring their own equipment or rent some from the local shops. It would have been an odd sight to see, but this was not a typical evening. It was an eventful night caused by peculiar people, to the point that nothing was surprising. Even the sight of two men wearing formal attire while strolling through the woods didn't raise any eyebrows. No one was nearby to question them, nor would anyone have dared to if they were. The gentlemen were not to be trifled with.

Trousers and a button-up shirt have never been considered to be proper hiking equipment, but that didn't stop Tartarus from making his way farther down the trail. His navy blazer had several cuts from the sharp branches that scrapped him as he walked by. Gloved hands carried a bone blade that was coated in a hardened black matter exactly like the one he used earlier in the night. The classy brown dress shoes he wore were covered in mud, and his tie was undone due to the heat. Any bit of his suit that was blemished quickly rectified itself. Cuts would stitch themselves together. Mud and other debris slid off the suit after enough time passed. Even the mask he wore was in perfect condition. Each golden gear on his navy mask continued to tick mechanically, winding the mainspring that covered his right eye before releasing the tension. Despite this mask covering his face, Tartarus didn't seem out of breath.

Erebus followed shortly behind his partner, but he seemed in a much worse condition. His bulkier figure was sharpened by the tailored formal outfit he wore. Midnight slacks reached down his legs, stopping just before his muddied dress shoes. A white button-up shirt hugged his torso. His amber sports coat had several tears along the arms, but the strands of fabric had already begun to intertwine together again. Following the trend of his fellow Evolved, Erebus wore an interesting mask that clashed with his otherwise fair outfit. The mask started as a basic blank bronze mask that covered his face. Welded to the mask was a shorter diamond-shaped plate which, presumably, held the mechanism that altered his voice. A darker masquerade mask had also been fastened to the base and frilled outwards. The mask's eye holes had been properly cut out and covered with a dark film. The right eye was hidden by a large camera lens which occasionally extended several inches before retracting. It was unclear whether he controlled its movement or benefitted from the mechanism. Etchings of film reels filled the remaining empty space of the mask.

"This is bullshit," Erebus complained in a robotic tune. The voice modifier continued to alter his voice beyond recognition. Even though his voice sounded like it came out of a radio that was in desperate need of repair, Tartarus had no trouble understanding him. Erebus leaned on a tree as he tried to regain his breath. He would never remove the mask he wore while working, but it did restrict his breathing a bit. To rub it in, the mask altered his heavy breathing as he gasped for air.

"You're killing me. A light jog like that was enough to knock you out of commission?" Tartarus chuckled as he moved on. He had no intention to wait for his partner who was practically pulling himself along. Compared to his companion, Tartarus showed no sign of exhaustion. He proceeded through the forest without any hesitation. Any obstacle in his way met the end of his blade as he walked toward their next target.

"Seeing how we ditched the car sixty miles ago because of traffic, I think you're the weirdo here. Give me some slack. Not everyone can run like you," Erebus panted heavily as he followed his partner. While the two were noticeably well-built men, Tartarus was leaner than his counterpart. Erebus's heavier physique was better suited for the fights the two were bound to get into throughout the night. On the other hand, Tartarus was better built to be the main hunter or pursuer.

"I guess the armored battalion is only good at one thing, huh? We should have gotten Nyx or Eros to deal with this. They would have done it faster than us," Tartarus chuckled. He may have been more agile than his friend, but he was far from the quickest of all Evolved. That fact didn't bother him though. Each Evolved was different and specialized in various areas. Everyone had a role to play. As the assault battalion commander, Tartarus knew his role.

"You know we can't bother them. Eros is on the other side of the country dealing with his own targets and issues. As for Nyx, we can't bother her before she's activated. Like it or not, we have to deal with this on our own," Erebus explained as he recovered. His breathing slowly stabilized as the conversation continued.

"I'm sure Nyx would be more than happy to have a warm-up target. She would be here in a heartbeat if *you* called." Tartarus said, mocking his friend. A grin appeared beneath his mask. He knew why Erebus was hesitant to call Nyx.

"We're already here, so just drop it." Erebus stepped ahead of Tartarus. He wanted to end the conversation before he was hassled again. His current situation wasn't favorable, and his friend loved to poke fun at that fact.

"You know, it is a major night that has the possibility of death for any of us. You can admit you're worried about your wi—" Tartarus stopped speaking immediately. He saw his partner's hand signal. They had finally arrived at their destination.

The two crouched to conceal themselves as the dense forest suddenly stopped. They stayed where the trees were to remain hidden. The edge of nature marked where the preservation ended. There was an obvious gap between an untouched environment and the encroaching immigration of new citizens. Only a few houses were present, but the skeletons of many more were in the process of being erected.

A sizable wooden cabin rested ahead of the two. It was the only complete building that matched the description of their target. Fortunately, it wasn't the same as the other matching houses in the area. The pinewood used to construct the home was noticeably different from the material that formed the other buildings. Smoke billowed from its chimney, and the windows were lit from the flickering flame. The chained swing rocked with the wind. A lovely scent of cooked sweets filled the air. Everything about the building showed that someone was there.

Erebus and Tartarus watched the ornate door in silence as it creaked open. A lone elderly woman holding a steaming coffee mug stepped outside. As she sipped her coffee, the two glared at her. She was their target and was clearly ready for their arrival. This seventy-year-old woman was equipped with high-end armor. Her thin figure was bulked by a prominent vest. Steel-toed boots, combat gloves, and knee and elbow guards protected her extremities. Gaps between the armor were covered in several layers of clothes, but it was obvious they were also advanced in some way. She pulled her white hair into a bun to prevent it from bothering her. Piercing yellow eyes stared back at the men that thought they were hidden. Her arms reached toward the porch's roof. After a few seconds of working with something, the woman pulled her weapon down. Her 12-gauge shotgun was primed and ready to remove the unwanted guests.

"I see you bastards!" the woman exclaimed before unloading a warning shot toward the two. The shot crashed into the ground between Tartarus and Erebus. Neither seemed worried about the woman's weapon. They didn't even flinch when shot at and began approaching her. Of course, a direct hit would cause some type of damage, but their determination was unwavering. The two parties glared at each other while they commenced their final conversation.

"It's about time you stopped running. Do you have any idea how hard it was to track you? I assumed you would stand your ground, but evading us was probably your best chance for survival," Erebus heckled the woman. He exaggeratedly flapped his coat, removing some of the mud that had yet to fall off. The leaves and grass beneath him waved as his motion sent gusts downward. Even with a gun pointed at him, he didn't see the need to be serious.

As the armored commander, the weapon was a feeble last resort.

Normal means of attack were almost pointless to use on him. His continuous healing and superior defense, even among Evolved, were what boosted his confidence. Erebus and his battalion were the shields of the night's operation. They were designed to withstand the strongest attacks. They were protectors of those weaker than them. It was up to them to act as a wall against any type of resistance and safeguard those that prioritized their targets. In Erebus's eyes, that is what it meant to be a part of his battalion.

"Well, I'm here now. It's a shame you didn't bring more of your kind. I was under the assumption my execution would be done by all of the commanders. I'm somewhat hurt that you don't think I'm worth their appearance." The woman pumped her shotgun. She aimed at the men and readied her next shot. "Come at me you damned Evolved!"

Erebus cocked his head toward the woman. He moved to oppose the need for all commanders to kill her, but Tartarus held his arm out. The attention shifted to him as he stepped forward. He knew this was a serious fight. This woman was confident for a reason. He just needed to know why. Unfortunately, his emotions began to get the better of him. Her casual remarks about the other commanders irritated him. She was responsible for all of their pain. Tartarus trembled as he voiced his opinion of the woman that stood before him.

"General Irina Quinn. You are the one that spearheaded the movement to alter us from our original forms. You are the one that specified the hellish training and modifications that we went through. You standardized and categorized us. You altered the five of us even further to better suit your 'Commander' role." Tartarus's voice quaked as he spoke. Every accusation fueled his rage further. His anger continued to boil over while he pointed his sword at her. Not even the mask he wore could hide the hatred that radiated from him. He pushed one of his legs back and assumed a running stance. "You are the one that ordered the execution of any Evolved that didn't meet your requirements. Worst yet, you are the one that organized the assassination of our original creators, Doctor Vivian Hathaway and Doctor Xander Schmidt. This night is retaliation for what you have put us through. So, face your judgment!"

Tartarus launched himself toward Irina at a blinding speed. Erebus quickly followed behind. Irina had a delayed reaction but was able to fire off a shot. Her startled slug missed its target, but she readied another before her assailants could reach her. Tartarus slowed his pace as the second shot was fired. Erebus leapt ahead of his partner. He crossed his arms to block the bullet and absorbed the impact of the shot, heavily reducing his overall speed. He tripped over himself as he tried to regain speed. Tartarus knew his friend was fine and refused to stop. With his run unimpeded, Tartarus was able to close the gap between him and Irina. She was unable to prepare another round before the blade reached her neck. A swift cut was all that was needed to lop off her head in one attempt.

But the blade suddenly stopped before it could end her life.

Blood dripped from where the edge nicked her flesh. An obsidian hand pinched the sword, restricting its movement. The hand was connected to a large mass of equally dark matter which slithered out from behind Irina. The blob of black slime began to morph and contour its body into a more human shape. Several layers of Irina's armor slipped away as the creature pulled itself together. Once the silhouetted person had finished forming, it snapped the blade between its fingers. Tartarus was too stunned to react, so the shaded person was able to throw a straight punch. Its strength was overwhelming and sent Tartarus flying into Erebus.

"I'm sorry. You haven't had the pleasure of meeting my new acquaintance. He's the newest development in the Evolved series. Prototype Delta was designed to be much better and adaptable than their predecessors. Of course, that includes your commander units. We're thinking of marketing these units under the name Dread. What's your opinion?"

Irina stated with confidence. She knew she was never in any danger, yet she strung the two men along the entire time. Her attempted attackers got up and assumed a defensive posture. Neither was seriously hurt, but the new situation had them on edge.

While normal weapons struggled against most Evolved, interspecies fighting could get deadly quickly. Information and tactics were what decided these types of encounters. This put Tartarus and Erebus at a severe disadvantage. Irina knew everything about them and likely relayed her information to Delta. Meanwhile, the two didn't know the first thing about the shaded enemy. Delta's category wasn't clear and the extent of their ability was also unknown. The masked men readied for the genuine battle they were about to have.

"You're one of the few that we couldn't get out, huh?" Tartarus tilted his head down. Delta didn't move. Their unisex form hadn't flinched since returning to a neutral stance. They stood still like a mannequin. "It's not too late. You can't stop us, so come with us. Live a life outside of the walls that cage you," Tartarus pleaded. He didn't want to kill one of his own, but his plea fell on deaf ears. Delta could only stare forward and wait. A sharp snapping sound seemed to trigger them into a rage, and they threw themself into Tartarus and Erebus.

"Did you honestly think I'd employ a unit that could be convinced against me? All Dreads have been preprogrammed to only follow their master's orders. Anything else falls on deaf ears," Irina chucked as the fight began. She aimed her firearm and readied her shot. The vanguard would occupy the assailants while she picked them off.

Delta's arms shifted and expanded before ramming into Erebus. The spurs that formed along their arms pierced their target's skin during the heavy swing. It took no effort to launch him away. As Tartarus looked at his friend being tossed aside, he was assaulted by a shot from Irina. Her aim was slightly off, but she was able to clip his shoulder.

The slug lodged itself in Tartarus and threw him off balance. He was surprised by the amount of pain that filled him. Writhing in agony was the only thing he could do as he processed what happened. His arm went limp, and the burning sensation began to radiate throughout his body. He had never felt this level or type of injury. The shot felt like it was poisoned. Tartarus's arm shook before locking. He rose unsteadily and moved closer to Erebus, who was evading Delta.

The two staggered back and regrouped. Their coats were torn and weren't repairing themselves, so they removed them. Moderate protection from that layer had less of an effect against other Evolved and whatever Irina was using. Blood spilled from them both as their bodies felt more rigid. Erebus wasn't hit with a shot like Tartarus, but something about Delta's attack started to gnaw at him. Irina sneered as she aimed at her targets. The masked men lost a significant portion of their confidence, and it showed. They needed to change tactics if they wanted to survive.

With his sword lost, Tartarus needed another weapon. He pushed up his damaged sleeves to free his arms. He flicked his only mobile arm downward, and dark matter burst from his elbow. The unnatural liquid rushed toward his hand and completely covered it. Small patches of blood flowed alongside several additional layers. After enough material had gathered, the structure hardened, aside from the joints. The crystalized claws that covered his hands were grotesque and made for an effective weapon.

Similar crystals formed around Tartarus's wound. Moments passed before he rotated his arm, shattering the newly formed bio-gems. His injury had fully healed, but the sluggishness didn't go away. He flicked his fixed arm to extend another jagged claw. It was noticeably smaller than the one previously formed, but that was to be expected. A good portion of the matter that created his claw went to his wound. More time needed to pass for his body to create more.

Erebus took the initiative as well. He seemed angrier than Tartarus and tore off the sleeves that were unable to protect him. Delta's single blow tore through two layers of advanced clothing and his superior defense. The situation felt like a pebble fighting a mountain. Erebus couldn't comprehend the strength his enemy had, but he refused to admit defeat. His title of armored commander couldn't be blemished any further.

Erebus widened his stance and held out his arms. The blood that poured from his wounds began to mix with a shaded liquid as it encompassed his body. The amalgamated fluid continued to cover him, moving under his clothing and around his head. With his body fully concealed, the coating agent hardened and formed interesting patterns. They were etched into Erebus's armor and looked like scales on a reptile. Several Greek symbols were also etched into the covering at random points on his body.

Both Delta and Irina seemed patient enough to allow all of this to happen. Maybe it was confidence or ignorance, but they stood back all the same. They weren't fazed by what they witnessed. It almost seemed like they were eager to start the real battle. Irina aimed her shotgun at Erebus. She wanted to see the extent of her weapon's power. Delta assumed an animalistic stance, waiting for the order to kill. Once the commanders of the armored and assault battalions were ready, the fight resumed.

Delta rushed toward the two while Irina fired her next shot. Erebus was able to absorb the impact, but it knocked him off balance. Reeling backward, he prepared to be bashed by the anomalous Evolved. A violent blow landed directly onto Erebus's chest, but it wasn't as detrimental as the first one. He was able to endure the hit, pushing his leg back to maintain the weight of Delta's arm.

Tartarus ran around the two, slashing at Delta's heels as he breezed by. The torn Achilles tendons frayed and squirmed. The dark matter slowly reconnected itself as Tartarus turned to attack again. He sliced into his target's back. The material that shielded Delta offered some resistance to the razor-sharp claws, but it wasn't enough. A thunderous roar could be heard as they twisted their body in an unnatural motion. Without moving their legs, Delta was capable of turning their torso around and backhanding Tartarus.

The nice wooden porch that offered a warm welcome to guests was shattered to pieces as Tartarus crashed into it. He quickly stood up and covered his face. Another shot rang out from Irina who intended to blast his head clean off, but it was stopped. In return for stopping the intimidating bullet, Tartarus had to sacrifice one of his claws. His proxy shield shattered upon impact. Pain coursed through his body from losing such a significant part of himself. Adrenaline pushed him forward as he charged at Irina.

Seeing the direct attack, she jumped back and readied the next round. A mask was between her crosshairs. Her finger pulled the trigger. Time slowed as the anti-Evolved shot flew through the air. Tartarus could almost see the slug getting closer. He gritted his teeth and adjusted his body. He knew he couldn't avoid it. Another sacrificed claw was needed to save him, but that would leave him defenseless and without a weapon. He didn't have time to debate the pros and cons of every possible action. Tartarus raised his already injured arm. He intended to ruin the already damaged limb to save the operable one.

However, a new combatant entered their field of view. It was impossible to ignore due to its position and posture. Tartarus thought his savior had arrived.

It only took a quick glance to know that was partially true. Erebus didn't intend to be hurled at such an extreme velocity, but he did use Delta's strength to his advantage. He used one of the massive attacks to propel himself into the fray and protect his friend. His body contorted in the air as he readied himself to take the bullet. There was just enough time to throw up two middle fingers and a death glare at the woman who shot it.

The slim slug packed quite the punch and managed to crack the armor that protected Erebus's ribs. It dug into his body but stopped midway. The shattered armor liquified and crystalized around the wound. The injured area was a prime target, but it was now several layers thicker than before. A burning sensation lingered around the bullet as though it were made of hot iron. Without time to think about the damage, Erebus continued sailing through the air. He broke into the home's wall and entered the building.

"*That idiot.*" A wide smile grew under Tartarus's mask. He silently thanked his friend for the opportunity. The ravenous claw opened. It thirsted for blood and set its sights on Irina. There was no hesitation in him. Tartarus dashed forward, putting all of his strength behind a massive strike. A war cry escaped him as he got closer to his target. Irina was unprepared for such an odd interruption, so her weapon was left uncocked.

Unfortunately, his target wasn't alone. Tartarus had tunnel vision and forgot about Delta. The creature also tossed itself into the situation. They wouldn't allow any harm to come to their master. Tartarus felt like he was hit by a freight train when Delta collided with him. The two tumbled into the broken home, landing near Erebus.

Delta rolled on the floor, using the momentum to hammer Erebus. There wasn't enough time to dodge, so Erebus took the brutal strike and winced from its crushing force. He could feel his armor breaking further, and the bullet lodged itself deep into his body. Erebus refused to allow that attack to go unpunished. He grabbed the arm that rested on him and pulled with all his might. His action wasn't forceful enough to pull Delta, but the maneuver wasn't intended to do so.

It was meant to provide an opening.

Tartarus dove over the two on the ground and sliced at Delta's trapped arm. The serrated claw cut through the black matter with ease. Each strand of the material frayed in the air. It was too deep of a wound to rapidly heal like before. Once the damage had been done, Erebus pulled even more. Delta's roar mixed with the sound of several fibers snapping. They had to resist. Their free arm moved to protect its weaker, almost removed, cohort. Tartarus again moved toward Irina. The sounds of struggle behind him grew as Delta tried to save its arm. Just like Tartarus before, Delta's vision grew too narrow.

It leaned in too deep and intercepted a shot intended to kill Erebus. Irina didn't think Delta would move to preserve itself. Why would it? She didn't give it that order. Tartarus was approaching her. It should have known to protect her. Instead, Delta was busy saving itself. Irina's brow furrowed as she realized her mistake. This prototype had the same issue as every Evolved that came before it had: it was too human.

Now there was one of those hellish bullets inside her subordinate. It was an unfortunate accident that dismantled her front line. Of course, any bullet from this firearm would injure Delta to some degree, but this shot was different. It was a developmental model of anti-Evolved weaponry. Irina didn't bother to understand the science behind it. She just needed to know if it could produce results. Based on how Delta's obsidian flesh sizzled around the wound, the bullet was a resounding success.

A bloodcurdling cry echoed as the pain set in. The other Evolved hit with similar shots could sympathize, but it was difficult to fully understand. They understood the basic concept behind the bullets. Each shot felt like it ate away at an Evolved's black matter: their ichor. The burning sensation spread like wildfire within their bodies. Fortunately, they were adaptable. An Evolved's body would restrict access to the remaining ichor supplies until the issue was resolved. In other cases, the ichor was mixed with enough blood to dilute it and prevent its dissolution.

Delta had neither of those two features. The ichor that covered their body couldn't prevent the poison's spread. It was nothing like the inner workings of an Evolved that could heavily adapt to survive. Delta's covering was like a field of dry grass ready to be burned. There was also a limited amount of blood they could use to diminish the ichor. The ratios were too far off to protect everything.

Erebus had seen enough. He tackled the writhing monster. No amount of strikes would finish off, so he needed a new type of attack. Time was running out. Delta would soon toss him aside. Erebus clenched his fist and braced for an extreme amount of pain. He pressed against the protruding wound where the bullet was housed. Agony coursed through him as fractures appeared along with the structure. The crystallized blood and ichor shattered after enough pressure was applied. The item that ate away at him burned his hand as he gripped it. He used one hand to hold Delta steady and his other readied the final attack. A swift punch wouldn't have been enough to end the beast, so all of Erebus's strength went behind the open–palm strike. The bullet was lodged directly into Delta's head.

The embedded object immediately spread its poison. Ichor dripped from the melting body. Vapors rose from the panicking creature. It rolled on the ground and scratched at its face, but the bullet was deep in the sea of ichor. The beast cried as the inky goop painted the floor. Any fibers that remained intact writhed on the ground before curling. Delta attempted to slither away, but there was nowhere to run. There was no remedy for their affliction. There was only mercy from the hands of Erebus. He stepped behind the shell of a monster and raised his foot.

A heavy stomp crushed Delta's skull with extraordinary power, and peace was finally brought to the agonized person.

Irina was left alone. Fear flashed across her face as she saw her subordinate fall. She dropped her empty shotgun and retrieved a sidearm. Erebus rushed her, taking two shots to the chest. His armor cracked further with each direct hit. He abruptly stopped several feet in front of her but not in pain. He brought himself down to one knee and covered his chest. Tartarus used his friend as a ramp, leaping toward his target with an open claw. He pushed against his friend to gain an extra burst of speed. Irina didn't have enough time to react before the arm that wielded her pistol was torn off. The collision sent her spinning toward the ground while her assailant landed several feet behind her. She got up with fear and anger covering her entire demeanor. Wild animals are always the most dangerous when they are cornered, and Irina was no exception. She bared her teeth and pulled out a small violet knife as her last resort.

She turned to Tartarus, who had thrown her arm aside. She let out a bloodcurdling scream before lurching forward. Her eyes were fixed on her target through the hair that fell forward. The eyes of a predator ready to pounce were enough to intimidate Tartarus, who was hesitating. He didn't want to move. Not from fear; it was because he didn't want to ruin his friend's plan. Erebus silently stepped toward Irina. The wood beneath him creaked, but nothing changed. She was too focused on Tartarus to notice. The two continued to glare at each other as Erebus approached his target. He used a sweeping kick to knock over the deranged woman. He avoided her slashes and put her into a rear-mounted headlock.

The two wrestled on the ground as Irina attempted to escape the death grip. Unfortunately for her, she couldn't overwhelm the superior strength of an Evolved. She wasn't the type to lose gracefully, so Irina began to kick, scream, and bite at Erebus. Her remaining arm firmly grasped the short blade in her palm and repeatedly stabbed it into her captor's side. The knife provided Erebus with a new feeling he hadn't felt in a long time: pure agony. Each stab caused such an immense amount of pain. It felt like multiple poisonous shots landed in the same area. One bullet put his body under significant stress, so these rapid attacks were brutal. He wanted nothing more than for the burning sensation to end. With Irina's head in both hands, Erebus let out a primal roar before snapping her neck. His victim immediately went limp and slumped to the floor.

"Erebus!" Tartarus blurted out. He had never heard his friend shout in pain like that. He rushed to his partner's side, punting Irina's corpse away. He looked at the stab wounds and noticed the knife was still embedded in its victim's side. The area around each injury had wide patches free from ichor. The eroded armor disintegrated in odd uniform patterns resembling computer wiring more than blood vessels.

An Evolved's body was built to withstand damage and adapt to any condition that may threaten it, but Tartarus didn't have time for his friend to slowly alter himself. There was no guarantee that the change would come quickly enough. He used his claw-free hand to break away the pieces of armor that crumbled away. Each snap of the shell forced Erebus to wince.

"F—fair to say I was th—the fight's MVP, huh?" Erebus tried to joke around. His hazy mind had a difficult time forming complete sentences. Losing ichor was akin to losing blood. As the venom ate away at him, he felt his mind drift away. Any excess energy had gone to the production of what he lost. This was on top of the blood he lost from the multiple stab wounds.

"Yeah. You had some good moments," Tartarus snickered as he continued to maintain his friend. His hands moved quickly along the armor, snapping off pieces that seemed toxic. He didn't want to take any chances and broke off more pieces than necessary. Tartarus was worried about Erebus accidentally absorbing contaminated ichor or blood. Satisfied, he gave his friend the thumbs up.

"N—nice. B—bet the little ones would be happy to hear that." Erebus's speech was slightly better. The mixture of blood and ichor slowly liquified. It flowed toward the wounds he had and reentered his body. The open injuries closed and crystallized once everything was back in place.

"Sure, but you seem to be out of commission now. I doubt you'll recover in time." Tartarus knew that ichor generation took several hours, if not days. Erebus was in no condition to continue the night. He couldn't maintain his armor, so he would just be a hindrance in the field.

"F—figures. She won after all," Erebus griped about losing. There was an ongoing bet among the Evolved about who would become the most recognizable figure from the night. Who would the human's latch onto? Who would they forget about immediately? Of course, they wanted to leave an impression for the entire species, but individual recognition would be appreciated. While it was meant to be a competition, most knew who would be the top contenders.

"Finally conceded, huh? It's not like she wouldn't have won anyway. Her job is to give the final message to the public. You were bound to lose. So, she gets to pick the kid's name now, right?" Tartarus rested next to Erebus. The remaining crystalized claw liquified and returned to his body. He cradled his head in his hands and stared at the ceiling. Yes, he did have more targets to get to, but that wasn't on his mind. The past few months were full of non-stop preparation for tonight. With such an important target eliminated, he deserved a bit of rest. No one would blame him for taking a few minutes to recover from the loss of his claw.

"Guess so. Oh well, Cassiopeia isn't the worst name in the world." Erebus assumed the same relaxed position his friend did. An excuse to rest wouldn't fly past without him taking advantage of it. The two felt relaxed in the ruined home. A gentle breeze flowed through the shattered entryway.

"It fits the theme with the other three. However weird it is," Tartarus chuckled. He knew of Erebus's children. They were good kids but born young and in this wild world. It wasn't uncommon for many of the Evolved participating in the night's events to have children. The entire population managed to escape their holding facilities over several years. Of course, there were also experiments involved in producing Evolved children. Erebus was fortunate. He was able to meet the love of his life and have children as a normal family would. A set of twins filled his heart with nothing but love and determination, and the third was a welcome surprise. He wanted nothing more than for them to live great lives. One that he would forge by risking his own. With a fourth little one planned in the future, it only filled the father with more motivation.

"What can I say? The stars mean something to me. I don't know what it is, but I want my kids to have that same connection," Erebus grinned. He loved talking about his children. Each of their milestones was meticulously documented. He did worry about smothering them with affection, but it was difficult to control himself.

All Evolved were subject to this sort of situation. The reason was simple: none of them had parents. They didn't know what it meant to have a child. Biologically, of course, there was no issue. Every support-type Evolved could explain the nutritional and educational needs of a child. The problem stemmed from the ways to raise and mold a young mind. There was no right way to do so. Many Evolved stayed together to help each other during these early stages of their species. The saying "it takes a village to raise a child" finally made sense to them all.

"You're a weird one, but I understand. The night sky was an amazing sight when I first got out. I couldn't tell you the constellations though. Just the zodiac ones you taught me." Tartarus struggled to comprehend his friend's fascination with the stars. He was aware that some type of experiment wiped out Erebus's memories, but the details were well hidden. There was also no record of his presence in any of the facilities that the other Evolved escaped from. Everything about him was confidential to the point that even he didn't know about himself. Erebus was unsure if he went through the procedure to become a commander, but it was assumed he did due to his abnormally high defense and intellect.

Erebus silently rose to his feet. His mind was still hazy but not enough to hinder his evacuation. Fighting was out of the question, so he needed to leave. He walked over to Irina. Her lifeless body rested near the monster she created. Erebus didn't bother with formalities when he confirmed her death. He dug through the pocket to retrieve a set of keys. A single click caused the car outside to honk.

"It's about time I head out of here." Erebus gripped his mask. The solid covering clanked as several internal latches snapped open. It came off easily when he pulled it over his head. Short brown hair fell from its compressed form. His skin was tanned, and his hazel eyes shone in the moonlight. He was incredibly handsome, similar to a Latin celebrity. Erebus had reverted into a human to mask his identity. He tossed his mask over his shoulder. "I'll be taking the car since you just *love* running around. Stay safe Tartarus."

"Yeah. You too Ere—" Tartarus began before stopping himself. It wasn't right to call a 'human' by some odd name. "Rest easy, Orion."

6

9:00 P.M.

In just a matter of hours, the nation had been brought to its knees. Reports and attacks continued to flood in every minute. Stories of horrifying experiences reached everyone's ears as a wave of fear flooded anyone that heard them. "What if I'm next" was a question that had been asked too many times to count. No one, except the targets themselves, knew about the Evolved's true intention. They knew the advanced humans existed, and their knowledge meant they were potential targets. In a bystander's eyes, however, the targeted individuals were chosen at random. This apparently lottery-like selection put society on edge. Trust in one another quickly diminished as everyone tried to fend for themselves. Many families remained in their homes while brave, or foolish, souls wandered the streets to meet the monsters.

The Evolved were already becoming known for their physical and mental superiority. Their ability to summon advanced weaponry or augment any part of their body also added to their threatening image. These were starling features, but it was not what people worried about. Blending in with the crowds they scared was the key attribute of the Evolved that sent civilians spiraling into madness. Distrust rose from the cracks as each assault further shattered people's social norms. Fear spread through individuals as they faced their mortality.

Police officers struggled to maintain public order as these attacks continued. It was nearly impossible for them to predict where the next one would happen. Some targets stepped forward, but they were swiftly eliminated despite the provided protection. Any exposed Evolved they chased would always manage to escape. Even if officers could catch up to them, conventional weapons had varying effects, but it was never enough. Restraining these Evolved was definitely not an option. Without the proper equipment, the police force was no different from normal civilians.

Enough time had passed to allow the mobilization of large military forces. The National Guard rapidly dispatched units to several cities and were combating the Evolved menace. Of course, it wasn't a perfect solution. Most Evolved could handle a full-size company, so the smaller forces that were deployed quickly diminished. It would take larger quantities of soldiers or more advanced munitions to fight them off effectively. They were able to eliminate a few wounded Evolved, but it wasn't near enough to save the night.

At least, that's what First Lieutenant Wallace Grant thought to himself. He was roaming the streets with his platoon, searching for survivors. The destroyed city was the result of panic once an Evolved appeared near the town hall. Reports indicated that the perpetrator was a short man dressed in formal wear. An odd block-shaped helmet covered their head, so it was impossible to identify him once he fled. The man was designated as a ranged-type Evolved due to his usage of a large bow and spined arrows.

This is where the nation's communication network shined. Every organization that was participating took initiative to spread any shred of information they gathered. The four identified commanders were used as a labeling system to better understand different Evolved types. After their identification, every Evolved was also designated by their assumed battalion: assault, armored, support, and ranged. This system allowed defensive forces to prepare for their area's assailant. Combat against them went in the human's favor sometimes as certain tactics proved efficient.

Many military groups were able to ward off the identified Evolved, but most of them were involved in the cleaning process of the attack's aftermath. Wallace and his team were one of the thousands that spent their night securing areas and assisting assaulted individuals. Each attack brought new orders to them. Their latest directions were the most critical. The Evolved man was severely wounded, and Wallace's platoon was to eradicate him before he could recover.

This group of soldiers spent almost an hour searching for one person. It was fortunate that their target wore an audacious helmet that made him stand out. The Evolved that ravaged the city was eventually found facedown in an alleyway. His body was riddled by gunfire from the last person it attacked. Higher caliber rifles had a difficult time penetrating an Evolved's defenses, and his injuries were on a different level. Not even his superior regeneration would allow him to recover against whatever ate away the black matter that protected him. There were too many of these types of injuries to repair. The Evolved stood no chance against it. Even an armored Evolved would have perished from such an attack. To show the extent of the damage, the infamous self-repairing suit was unable to stitch itself together. The people that found the body breathed a sigh of relief.

The platoon was reasonably concerned about approaching the corpse. All of the Evolved were being considered to be ultimate anomalies, so no one knew it was safe to approach their deceased bodies. For all they knew, the cadaver was rigged to explode. Nevertheless, they needed to confirm the man's death. Fifteen members of the team stayed with the vehicles and reported the sighting. The remaining half went with Wallace toward the body. They knew the risk when they entered the city, so they steeled themselves for the inspection point. Each step seemed calculated as they encircled their target. Rifles were readied and aimed at the corpse as they carefully stepped closer. Cold breaths escaped their lips as they prepared for the worst-case scenario.

Wallace had nothing to do but retrieve the body. He approached the corpse with absolute caution. Four additional platoon members walked behind him. They kept their weapons trained on the enemy as Wallace turned the body over. The full moon provided minimal light, so the surrounding soldiers' flashlights brightened the situation further. The boxed helmet was severely cracked, and a large shatter line reached from one corner to the other with plenty of branching arms accompanying it. The helmet was made of solid steel and had darkened unevenly, presumably from soot and debris.

The lieutenant struggled to fully twist the body and face it up. Each limb was unnaturally heavy, and the metal helmet didn't help during the procedure. Pride prevented Wallace from asking for help. He was a new officer, so he wanted to prove to his subordinates that he was worthy of their respect. It took all of his strength to flip the deceased man.

As the body turned over, the helmet cracked further. A loud thumping sound rang out as the heavy metal tipped to its side. Sparks flew around the area of impact, igniting small puddles of black liquid. The ignition didn't result in a grand explosion. Instead, it simply fizzled and crackled before completely burning out. Nevertheless, the team was startled. Fingers lightly grazed their triggers that held back a barrage of bullets. Had they not been properly trained, everyone would likely have fired in a panic. It was fortunate that they remained calm. With the most frightening moment past them, the team prepared the body for transport.

Of course, they were curious about the man beneath the mask, but it wasn't the right time to satiate their questions. Their job was to return the body to the rendezvous point designated by their commanding officer. A body bag was readied and covered the man. It took some finesse to cover the bulky helmet he wore, but they managed to do it. The weight of both the man and his helmet made it impossible to lift the bag. Several team members were required to move the body, but all they could do was assist in dragging it. The way they dragged the bag seemed disrespectful, but there was no alternative method to relocate it.

The group was making excellent progress and managed to drop their cargo into the large transport truck. Several team members sat next to the body, keeping their weapons at hand. The confirmation of his death didn't quell their concerns in the slightest way. Wallace accompanied the truck's driver, Staff Sergeant Tina Mitchell, and radioed their finding to the commanding officer. He confirmed their departure and alerted the platoon to move out. Every soldier present knew which of the four transport vehicles to be in. Engines revved as the convoy left the scene.

Wallace's truck was to drive in the middle of the vehicles for extra defense, but the vehicle didn't move when it was their turn to depart. Wallace and Tina looked around them. There was nothing visible that could have been holding them still. The engine roared as Tina urged it to move, but the truck wouldn't budge. Given their current circumstances, it was safe to assume an Evolved was halting their evacuation.

Everyone swiftly exited the vehicle and prepared for combat. Wallace scanned the area, but there was nothing particularly interesting. Tina jumped into the truck's bed to analyze the body. None of the soldiers there reported movement, but it was best to confirm for herself. She knelt down and felt the bag, debating whether to open it. Her hesitation allowed her to notice a glimmer of light by her feet. Meanwhile, the lieutenant stopped at the end of the truck to speak to Tina.

"Something wrong with the body?" Wallace asked. There should have been nothing on the body to note, but he still worried that he missed something crucial. It would have been embarrassing to make an oversight during this critical time. All eyes were on him to perform his duties and maintain morale. Needless to say, he felt the pressure tonight brought.

"Yes, there's . . ." Tina's eyes followed the glimmer that showed a thread. It was slightly larger than a spider's web and dark as night. She wouldn't have noticed it if the moonlight was any weaker. The line floated in the air as it extended away from the vehicle's bed. Her eyes widened as she noticed several other threads alongside the initial one. They were all connected to the truck and body. She moved to shout, but it was too late.

Something pulled the truck back with an aggressive amount of force. Wallace was swept into the truck and slammed onto the bed's floor. Loud cracks and snaps sounded as the vehicle reversed. Everyone in its path threw themselves out of the way and watched in horror. Wallace and Tina recomposed themselves and gripped the bed's edge. The other four soldiers remained in their seat and braced against the sudden force.

Tina was the first to take initiative and drew the knife that was fastened to her vest. She started to cut away at the thread. Wallace followed suit shortly after. Their collaborative effort made excellent progress until more threads appeared. They slithered into the truck and gripped it once again. Several strands approached the two who had removed them earlier. The hands that were their bane were now in their grip.

Each thread was thin, but its strength was unnaturally powerful. They wrapped around Tina and Wallace's hands before increasing the pressure. The vice grip tightened further, crushing their victims. The soft crunches of broken bones were drowned by the loud wind that rushed past them. The two tried to pull the ensnarement off, but that only allowed the substance to spread further.

The chaos continued for almost a minute before the truck suddenly stopped. They were previously accelerating at an intense speed, so the immediate stop forced everyone in the truck to go flying. Even the heavy body floated in the air as its momentum carried it away. As the soldiers tumbled, Tina and Wallace were yanked back. The threads that assaulted them were still attached to the truck. Everyone else landed in the remains of a collapsed building. The body landed in the center of them with an audible thud.

The restrictive fibers released their captives and slithered away. Wallace gripped his hands as the pain locked him in place. Meanwhile, Tina stood up and peered at her comrades. The presence of an Evolved was much more problematic than a crushed hand. It seemed like an act of kindness toward her fellow soldiers, but it was more akin to self-preservation. Everyone had a reason to survive the night. Tina's reason was her child. That little boy was always on her mind. He was the reason she continued to fight through the night and strive to live on.

As she glanced at those who were thrown off the truck, her view was filled with the source of the black threads. An enormous web stood in the wreckage of the building. Each connection point consisted of hundreds of strands, strengthening the web's integrity. This collection of strings continued throughout the web, giving it the girth of standard rope. It kept its angled position several feet above the ground like it anticipated the ones foolish enough to be ensnared by it. Much like a real spider's web, the threads were incredibly sticky and clung to everything that touched it. The four soldiers felt like flies waiting for their demise.

The two who managed to stay away from the trap readied themselves. It wouldn't take long for an Evolved to appear, and two injured soldiers wouldn't be able to put up much of a fight. Wallace equipped his sidearm while Tina picked up one of the loose rifles. Broken hands prevented them from using their weapons effectively. Tina propped her firearm onto the truck's edge to act as a stabilizing platform and increase her accuracy. Meanwhile, Wallace forced himself to steady his pistol with his forearm. In the few seconds they looked away to prepare, someone new appeared at the center of the web.

It was a tall, slender woman. She was standing on the web that trapped her prey, free from the unbreakable grip each thread had. A fully tailored forest suit sharpened her figure, and an interesting mask covered her face. The base of the mask was made from bort, expertly cut to follow the curvature of her head. Eight large emerald ellipses covered the eyes and forehead. It was clear that the headgear was composed entirely of gemstones that glistened in the moonlight. One could mistake it for fine art if it weren't attached to a monster. The mask would have been distracting enough on its own, but there was another aspect of her figure that drew attention away from the remarkable craftsmanship.

Outreaching from her back were four thick appendages, but they were nothing like normal limbs. Instead, they were a larger version of the string that formed the web. Their mobility was limited in exchange for increased power. She seemed to easily control these extremities as they extended from behind her. Her main body didn't move as her unnatural parts carried her forward. Careful steps were placed between the web's threads.

Wallace and Tina opened fire. The woman was essentially a sitting target, thanks to the outlandish limbs that held her up high. Unfortunately, she was anything but a defenseless target. Each bullet fired was easily deflected by her extraordinary reflexes. It took no time for the rear onyx appendages to catch the incoming projectiles and flick them away. The bullets were nothing more than an annoyance to her. To rid herself of the irritating pests, she struck the large truck. One of the limbs moved like a whip as it dashed through the air, and it crashed into its intended target with the force of a bus going sixty miles per hour.

The poor truck was sent flying, toppling onto its side. Its passengers were thrown into the air as their protection rolled into the web's edge. The vehicle was now the newest prisoner to be caught by the unbreakable lining. Following it shortly after was Tina, who collided with a group of cords. She felt their grip lock her in place. Even her absolute strength couldn't pry her off. Wallace landed near her, catching his foot on a high strand. The web clung to his boot, which eventually slipped off. He was free from its grip, but under the web wasn't a place he wanted to be. Through the threaded lines, Wallace could view the spider Evolved.

She was hunched over the two soldiers that rested next to the body. Her dainty hands reached out and tightly gripped their collars. The web was able to hold them despite their constant thrashing, yet the woman pulled them off with ease. She nonchalantly lifted the two above her head before tossing them outside of the web's range. With the insects removed from the immediate area, the Evolved turned to collect her prize. Thin fibers, similar to the ones that gripped the truck, extended from her jade sleeves. They carefully slid underneath the body bag and lifted it into the air. The strands danced in the moonlight as they brought the bag behind the woman. Her arms raised as they slid around both her and the bag, fastening the corpse to her back while still allowing freedom of movement.

She confidently stepped along her web and moved away from the soldiers. They watched with stunned expressions as she waltzed away. Half of the team was locked in place, and the other half was frozen in fear. The quote "choose your battles wisely" rang through them. Fighting an Evolved was already next to impossible. Their team was limited, and most of their weapons were either out of reach or stuck to the web. Tina knew better than to try an escape. Survival was her only goal, but Wallace was determined to prove his worth. Any kind of engagement would have resulted in death, so he chose an alternative route.

Wallace held his breath as he crawled forward. The web hung inches over his head. A single collision was all it would take to stop him in his tracks. He was forced to press himself down while pushing forward. It was a strenuous movement during an intense situation, but he didn't want to let the woman escape. He would do anything he could to show that he was a true leader. Even if it risked his life, Wallace needed to continue following the woman.

The spider Evolved was still in everyone's sight. She stepped along her web's path toward one of its connection points on the damaged building. Half of the enormous structure was collapsed and a mountain of debris cluttered the open area. It was fortunate that it was a simple storage facility. Wallace didn't want to think about the lives that would have been lost had this type of destruction occurred in a residential area. The woman's large appendages carried her as the terrain grew more jagged. She was able to enter the building with relative ease and dissolved into the shadows.

The lieutenant refused to give in. He hastened his pace, raising his body ever so slightly to gain a bit more traction. His old drills of crawling under barbed wire were never this intense. They never gripped his outer layer to the point that he'd need to abandon it, but this web was much different than any training exercise. Wallace eventually escaped from under the trap and scraped himself along the rubble of a shattered warehouse. He looked back to the two that also escaped the web, still frozen in fear.

"Call for reinforcements! Tell them we've engaged the enemy! Take extreme caution when removing the others from the web!" Wallace snapped his subordinates out of their daze. He wasn't always the perfect leader, but he did have his moments. He didn't expect them to follow after the Evolved. It was natural to run from such an unconventional adversary, but that didn't mean they could sit and do nothing.

If they refused to follow Wallace, then they can recover the others. If they recover the others, they might learn something about the dark threads. Information was how they survived this long. It was critical that they continued this flow of intel gathering. It could be the one thing that saves their lives or, at least, the lives of the next poor souls that get caught.

It didn't take long for Wallace to scale the small mountain and enter the building. His steps slowed as he looked around. All of the windows were shattered. The walls were either punctured or beaten in. The floors were crushed as if something had continually slammed against them. Splatters of blood and ichor colored the otherwise monotone room. Several squares made of tape were formed along the ground. Each one was the same size, precisely measured for some use. The reason didn't connect for Wallace, but he wasn't there to investigate the Evolved's absurd practices. He needed to find the woman and the body she had stolen.

As he continued to walk the building's length, the internal damage steadily increased. Wallace noticed that the mayhem was confined to the taped areas on the ground. It was almost impossible to see any more details due to the limited light. He resorted to using his flashlight but worried about exposing himself to the enemy. The line of sight scanned the ground before locking onto a set of metal doors. They were cold to the touch and heavy to push. It took a large amount of force to open the entrance. As it opened, the hunks of metal creaked and echoed through the empty room. Wallace was surprised that the doors weren't locked. A large stairway descended into the depths, far exceeding his expectations.

He took a breath before taking a step, only to immediately regret it. A thin rogue strand was hanging from the ceiling. It lifelessly brushed against the intruder's face, sending him into a panic. Wallace twisted and swiped at the presence. He slipped on the step as he fled from the false enemy. A valiant effort to catch himself was in vain as gravity pulled him down. He tumbled the length of the stairs in complete darkness. It was impossible to tell how long he fell or the number of steps he bumped into, but it eventually ended less than a minute later.

Wallace immediately rose to his feet. He looked around in a panic, trying to see through the darkness. His body followed the light that darted throughout the empty room. No creature could sneak up on him while he flailed like this. It only took a moment for him to realize he was standing in an empty hallway. Wallace's energy swiftly diminished. The perceived threat was nowhere to be found. He was safe, for the moment.

He waited several seconds before assessing the new area. Analytic eyes scanned the hallway, looking for any details that stood out.

The corridor continued for several yards before ending in another set of large metal doors. They were similar to the previous ones but with one glaring exception. The bottom of the steel opening had been forced upward. This barrier, which was several inches thick and designed to withstand an explosion, was crumpled like paper. Two prominent grip marks showed where the metal was forcibly pried from its original position. Wallace shuddered as he thought about the kind of Evolved that did this.

A soft blue light came from the other side of the door. There was an internal debate within Wallace about whether to enter the room. It took several moments to steel his resolve. He was forced to crawl once again. The movement wasn't as difficult, but there was still a level of fear. The spider Evolved could appear and attack him while he was in a vulnerable position. More threads may lock him in place. They were both good reasons to perform this motion as fast as possible. It was fortunate that he didn't run into anything as he swiftly crawled through the gap.

The room was lit with soft blue lights that radiated from behind the various shelves and drawers that lined the walls. Unblemished marble flooring spanned the room. The counters had several small sinks and burners separated by clear dividers. Everything about the room screamed laboratory, but there was no equipment to validate this assumption. The shelves and drawers were left bare. Not even the dust had settled in the grand room. Instead, it was systematically filled with tables that created a large grid.

The nine tables each held a large black canvas bag. They closely resembled the bags used to gather deceased Evolved. No, they were identical to those distributed by the military. It was safe to assume these were much like the block-headed Evolved from earlier, stolen from those that initially recovered them.

"A morgue?" Wallace mumbled to himself. He didn't intend to speak aloud, so the echoes startled him. He approached the closest bag. His breathing slowed as he noted the prominent cube in place of the corpse's head. A heavy foot tried to step closer but was caught by something on the ground. Wallace wavered as he was thrown off-balance. He fell forward and would have collapsed directly onto the body, but his fall was cut short by an odd force that caught him. It felt a lot like landing on a trampoline. The sensation would have bounced him upright if it didn't immediately latch onto him. He tried to free himself but to no avail.

"How observant," a mature feminine voice spoke. The sound came from above Wallace, but he couldn't move his head to see the woman. Even without witnessing her, Wallace knew she was the spider-like Evolved. She seemed to recognize her newest victim. "The soldier from the surface. Come to secure Quadrate's corpse?"

One of the woman's petite arms reached around Wallace. Her hands followed the contours of his figure. Wallace winced as she felt certain parts of his body. Had he not noticed his injuries? The woman stopped her hands and applied pressure to the wounds. Wallace felt his breath catch in his throat as the pain increased.

"Rudimentary analysis has completed. Left hand: broken. Left arm: fractured. Left clavicle: fractured. Left ribs five and six: fractured. Untreated injuries may worsen." She spoke in a monotone voice. Her robotic tone fell silent as she thought for a moment. The hands that scanned their target returned to the woman's side. She continued her analytical statement: "One moment. Medicine for human consumption is nearby."

Wallace expected to hear her footsteps leave, but there was no sound. She rushed away using the threads that hung from her back. Wallace didn't understand her intention and refused to wait for the woman to return. The strands that held him were thin, but their strength was unquestionable. He knew brute force wasn't an option. Shimmying out of the web was also impossible unless he wanted to remove some skin in the process.

All he could do was arch his back and pull away from the trap to prevent more contact points from being generated. His deep stretch was interrupted by a hand that wrapped around his jaw. The force pulled him further down, giving Wallace the feeling that his spine would snap. He tried to resist the force, but its strength was overwhelming. He opened his mouth to let out a cry, only to be silenced by a bottle.

"Drink the medicine," the woman said. She silently returned and watched her victim's actions. She knew nothing would change, but analyzing her prey brought a better understanding of how they resisted the web. A desire to comprehend humans almost drove a more in-depth investigation, but she restrained herself.

The woman's inhuman strength held the bottle still as Wallace shook his head. Streams of a crimson liquid poured from the corner of his lips. He tried not to swallow, but it was impossible to resist its flowing motion. The liquid's consistency was similar to honey and clung to his throat as it snailed through. Once empty, the woman removed the bottle and placed her hand over his mouth. Wallace could feel her threads stretch over his mouth, sealing it shut. He was left with no other option but to swallow the remaining fluid. The bitter taste of defeat and whatever was in the medicine remained when the liquid settled in his stomach. Satisfied, the woman peeled off the threads and stepped back.

"What was that?!" Wallace coughed. He wished he could eject what he just consumed. His stomach turned due to his worry about a potential poisoning.

"Nectar. A developmental medication for Evolved. This prototype recently finished processing. Further research is needed. How are you feeling?" The woman droned. She had an interesting speech pattern that forced shorter, more direct, sentences. Her interest in Wallace seemed genuine, but it was more aimed at his reaction to the medication rather than his well-being.

"What are you—" Wallace tried to angrily reply. His words were halted when he felt a wave of exhaustion hit him. His eyes grew heavy, and his vision blurred slightly. He tried to shift himself, getting into a more comfortable position. The web that trapped him slightly loosened its grip and lowered his body. It started to act more like a cushion than an unbreakable substance. As Wallace moved, he noticed the pain that once filled his chest was gone. His arms, collar, and hand all felt better as well.

"An Evolved," the woman responded. "Designation: Support Battalion Commander. Codename: Gaia. That is what I am." She answered the few words that left Wallace. The most basic identification details were given to him. It left him perplexed. The stunned man could only watch as Gaia walked toward the body he once tried to touch. She used her extra limbs to grasp some of the other nearby bodies around her and tie them together with her threads.

"A commander helping an enemy soldier? I knew the Evolved were odd, but this goes beyond reason," Wallace moaned in exhaustion. He couldn't comprehend why someone he needed to eliminate would assist him. The Evolved showed no mercy for their targets, yet they hesitated to harm anyone else. Of course, this fact didn't apply to all of them. Members of the support battalion were the most likely to show mercy while the ranged battalion showed little to none. This primarily stemmed from both differences in commanders and group mentality.

"Compassion is not exclusive to humans." Gaia continued to collect the bags and stitch them together. It didn't take long for two moderately sized chains to form. Each body was linked to another through a variety of thick and thin threads. The train of bodies followed Gaia as she casually stepped through the room.

"Then why tonight? Why do all this for your fallen friends?" Wallace could barely keep his eyes open. It was a struggle to stay conscious. He tried to reference her massive web and attack above ground, but Gaia latched onto a different word that was said.

"They are not Fallen. We are the Evolved. We are not monsters."

Wallace couldn't understand why the word 'fallen' gripped Gaia's attention. He wanted to ask for more information. The only thing that stopped him was his growing exhaustion. White noise filled his ears as he drifted to a loose state of mind. His consciousness slowly slipped away, but Gaia's final words were able to reach him. He closed his eyes as he processed what she said.

"Peace is all we desire. Spread our message. Rest easy, soldier."

7

9:30 P.M.

The night's attacks startled to dwindle in frequency as the day came to its final hours. Almost every target had been eliminated. The few that remained were still fleeing from their hunters, but it was only a matter of time before they would meet their end. Nearly all of the successful Evolved managed to escape and reenter society without notice. The less fortunate among them were either captured or killed. Luckily, a separate group of Evolved was tasked with retrieving their comrades, dead or alive.

These units were led by the newest identified commander: Nyx. This commander led the mobile battalion and left no room for doubt that she was the most agile of all Evolved. She was constantly evading pursuers and leading them astray while her subordinates performed their duties. Her extendable limbs were the perfect mix between grappling hook and slingshot, the best possible combination for traversing the concrete jungle. It took little effort for her to swing around the district and act as a distraction. Her playful attitude and mocking words only irritated her exhausted chasers.

The mobile battalion's actions were the last of the night's major events, so it was no surprise that humanity came close to bending its knee.

The knowledge gained helped, but each successful attack took a toll on morale and stamina. There was no way to match the monstrously endurant Evolved. The battalion was an interesting group. Much like the other battalions, this organization had a focus on one specific task and revolved around a basic group mentality. These mobile-type Evolved were noticeably swifter than their companions. Their combat strength varied, but they tended to avoid most kinds of confrontation. They focused solely on the recovery of their allies.

The people of the nation were finally able to catch their breath as the dust settled. Reports detailing each encounter began to spread like wildfire. News stations struggled with the surplus of stories they were expected to cover. It was impossible to go over all of them, so they chose to focus on the critical targets or large-scale massacres. Citizens from all walks of life tuned in to see the scope of the night that would go down in history. Everyone fell silent as more details came to light. Each account piled onto the fear that continuously grew.

The defeated tone of a field reporter echoed through a young woman's mind. She had been resting on the floor for what felt like hours, lying on her back with her limbs spread out. A puddle of drool had formed and stuck several strands of hair to her face. Her body was sluggish and felt abnormally heavy. It was the deepest sleep she'd ever woken from. The young woman struggled to stand without the support of a nearby desk. She rubbed her neck as she tilted her head, feeling the fractured surface of a dried liquid. Her mind was still in the process of waking up, but a single thought revived her.

"*Mom and dad!*" Violet worried about the well-being of her parents. She recalled the events that occurred before she was knocked unconscious. Thoughts of the two dangerous individuals filled her mind as she called out to her parents. She cried aloud to the empty house, but only the muffled voice of a news reporter responded. The silence gave Violent goosebumps. Her once lively home had never reached this hushed level.

All of the lights in the house were off, and the office was now a pit of darkness set to swallow Violet. Despair built in her heart as it pounded louder than ever before. Fear filled her mind as she imagined what horrible things could have happened to her parents. She gritted her teeth and smacked her cheeks lightly. She needed to motivate herself to move forward and have faith that her parents were safe. She wanted to believe that this was all a nightmare. She clung to the thought that the attack was unsuccessful, refusing to acknowledge that the Evolved were unstoppable.

"It was just some trick of the eye. It'll be alright. Dad's got a gun in the safe," Violet thought to herself. The idea brought solace to her otherwise deteriorating mind. Neither intruder wielded any type of weapon, so there was the possibility that her parents could have fought them off. If not, there was the chance that help came for them. They weren't unbeatable monsters. No problem didn't have an obtainable solution. Violet continued this train of thought as she entered the hallway.

The wooden floor creaked as she took each step. She tried to slow her breathing to calm herself, but to no avail. Every unpredicted noise caused Violet to flinch violently. The shaded corridor watched her as she crept toward the living room. A dim light was her only guide. The subtle illumination allowed her to see the large scratches that peppered the walls.

The light came from a flickering television resting on its back. The screen was partially broken, so a significant portion of the image was frozen. The channel continued to report on the night's events, but Violet tuned it out. She was too focused on her family's well-being. As Violet entered the large room, she took note of its condition.

The comfortable L-shaped couch that lined the far corner was empty. Its cushions were gutted and scattered across the room. The cozy blanket that once provided warmth was a shredded mess. The nostalgic dark-stained coffee table was flipped on its side. Shards of glass rested on the ground near the broken window, and the window's large curtain hung loosely in defeat. Everything about the room radiated the words "crime scene."

A thin trail of blood started from the couch's edge and flowed toward the kitchen. It likely came from a small cut. Violet thought of hypothetical answers that would result in the small spillage. She continued to entertain the idea that her parents were fine, but it became more difficult for her to do so as her eyes followed the trail. The stream thickened before halting at a large pool. It was clear that the woman's sneak attack was successful, likely damaging Ivan, who was in the room at the time. The preemptive strike wasn't enough to kill him but was not intended to. Judging by the scene, the assailant wanted to drag out the encounter. Violet continued to play the role of detective as she made her way into the next scene.

The kitchen was meticulously cleaned each night by Violet's mother, Claire. If she were to see its current state, she'd lose her mind. The walls were bashed and heavily scratched by monstrous means. Several dirty dishes rested in the sink, and the faucet continued to pour warm water. The blocked drain forced the water upward, creating a massive puddle on the tiled floor. The edge of the formation merged with the trail of blood that the amateur investigator was following.

Even with the helpful line gone, its endpoint was obvious. The master bedroom was a dark void that Violet was afraid to enter. The room's door was smashed open, as though a powerful kick had shattered the wood in two. Its top half was tossed aside, and the bottom hung loosely on its broken hinges. The wall around the door was heavily damaged. Most of the area was either caved in or had large gashes. Violet thought the intruders were somewhat composed, but the scenes she viewed looked more like an animal attack. She stepped forward with bated breath.

"*Their last stand,*" Violet thought to herself before she cleared her mind. She was hesitant to enter the room. Her hands wouldn't stop shaking, and she felt an ever-present chill. One step forward was all she could handle. The room's temperature dropped several degrees.

Second step.

The view was still obstructed by the door's frame.

Third step.

One more deep breath was needed.

Final step.

The room was now completely visible. The night's outcome was clear. Her parents lost their fight. A monster had entered and finished what it intended to do. Its victims rested on the large bed, now soaked in blood. An empty pistol rested on the ground beneath them, unable to protect its owners. The scene was a mess, and it took every bit of willpower for Violet to analyze the status of her deceased parents. She wanted nothing more than to turn away but had to see what happened.

Ivan was the worst of the two. His eyes were swollen shut from a series of blows. The rest of his face was bruised and cut. The weapon of choice must have been a blunt object with smaller sharp points affixed to it. Regardless of the exact tool, it left Ivan vulnerable and bleeding profusely after a few strikes. The rest of his body also suffered from similar wounds which showed the limited, yet deadly, arsenal the intruders had. Most of the injuries came from his resistance. Violet hated to admit it, but Ivan would have fared better if he had given up earlier in the fight.

Claire, on the other hand, was in relatively better condition. Her wounds were lighter. They mostly consisted of cuts and scrapes from being tossed aside multiple times. She tried her best to fight for her husband, resulting in her demise. Her lifeless eyes stared at the ground as she laid atop Ivan. Claire's final action was shielding him from the brunt of the final blow.

A large blade consisting of bone and dark matter skewered the two bodies.

Faced with the scene before her, Violet dropped to her knees. Any hope that once occupied her mind had now dissipated. Tears trickled down as she wailed in sorrow. The night's reality had been exposed, leaving the young woman broken. She cried for what seemed like an eternity. Her emotional pain continued to eat away at her and would do so for a long time. Violet was too devastated to notice the voice coming from behind her.

It was the living room's television. The field reporter was replaced by an unorthodox individual. This woman wore a tailored rose suit, and a helmet covered her head. The compressed motorcycle headwear had a brilliant gold visor. Etchings of a moon and constellations covered the otherwise bland areas. These gaps were filled with white to pop out against the deep red. If this woman was trying to be an obvious target, it was working. She held the microphone and spoke with unquestionable authority.

"Good evening. I am Nyx, leader of the mobile battalion. I come to you humans in one of the darkest moments of your history." The voice spoke directly to the audience rather than the network's hosts. She took a dramatic pause before continuing her speech. "We, the Evolved, have finally stepped into the light. We have shown you our power and the devastation that can come from it. Despite how you might perceive us, we wish to establish peace between our two species. However, to do that, we needed to rid the world of the people that created and tormented us. One thousand targets. All eliminated in a single night. This will go down in history as the night the Evolved liberated themselves. The night that we gained our freedom. The night where you recognized us. The night of a thousand blades."

Afterword

If you made it this far into the book, thank you. I'm Dominic Morales, the author of this peculiar series of short stories.

It has been an absolute blast making this book. This has been an interesting experience, to say the least. I'd never published a book before (much less do almost everything involved in it). A simple short story ended up turning into two then three. Before long, an entire book was formed around the debut night of the Evolved.

I can't go without saying a big thank you to my family. Without their feedback and opinions on the initial story, this book would have never been completed. You all are the best! Even the ones that didn't read it but still offered unwavering support.

I'd also like to thank my friend and cover artist, Jesse Painter. Your work on the cover was amazing, and I can't wait to work with you again on the next one.

So, what'll happen now? The story goes on. How will the next generation handle their new societal norm? Are there any concepts that haven't been covered yet? That's what I'm hoping to find out in the next book, which will be a full story rather than several shorter ones. I can't wait to get started!

Until then, thank you so much, again. I hope you'll continue reading.

See you then.

www.ingramcontent.com/pod-product-compliance
Lightning Source LLC
Chambersburg PA
CBHW070517200726
48293CB00007B/2582